PUFFIN BOOKS

Editor: Kaye Webb

HOBBERDY DICK

Long ago, long before our great-grandfathers were born
and before the ancient ways left our countryside, there
was plenty of secret folk-life in England, particularly
hobgoblins who guarded the houses and lands and
watched over the families who lived in them, until their
task was done and they were released. Th___ ___ins
were shy folk who stayed out ___ ___ so
determined and me___ ___ ___es
and dislikes. Happy ___ ___
woe betide anyone w___

Hobberdy Dick o___
was a good and car___ ___
who came in after the ___ ___ his affection
like the Culvers, whom ___ known and liked for two
hundred years. The Puritan city merchant and his spoilt
wife worked their servants hard and forbade all country
pleasures. There was no mumming or Maying, or Christmas dancing or Easter egg rolling now, and none of the
comfortable chat and fireside games that Dick had loved
in the past.

It seemed a hopeless outlook; Dick could only work by
stealth and there were such strong and wicked forces out
to damage the children, but Dick still saw hope for the
future – in Anne Seckar, the penniless cousin of the Culvers, and Joel, the merchant's eldest son, who loved the
country and the old ways. It was because of them that
Dick and his friends Taynton Lob, Patch, Hairy Tib and
old Grim saved young Martha from the witches' spell.

K. M. Briggs is a well-known authority on folk lore,
and Hobberdy Dick is so memorable and charming a
character that this book is very well worth reading, not
just for its wealth of magic and historical material but for
its fascinating story.

Cover design by Scoular Anderson

HOBBERDY DICK

K. M. BRIGGS

Illustrated by
Scoular Anderson

PUFFIN BOOKS

Puffin Books, Penguin Books Ltd, Harmondsworth, Middlesex, England
Penguin Books Inc., 7110 Ambassador Road, Baltimore, Maryland 21207, U.S.A.
Penguin Books Australia Ltd, Ringwood, Victoria, Australia
Penguin Books Canada Ltd, 41 Steelcase Road West, Markham, Ontario, Canada
Penguin Books (N.Z.) Ltd, 182–190 Wairau Road, Auckland 10, New Zealand

—

First published by Eyre & Spottiswoode 1955
Published in Puffin Books 1972
Reprinted 1976

—

Copyright © K. M. Briggs, 1955

—

Made and printed in Great Britain
Richard Clay (The Chaucer Press) Ltd,
Bungay, Suffolk
Set in Linotype Baskerville

To Katharine Kingshill

One

Wae's me, wae's me!
The acorn's not yet
Fallen from the tree
That's to make the cradle
That's to rock the bairn
That's to grow to a man
That's to lay me.

*The Cauld Lad
of Hilton's Song*

HOBBERDY DICK stared from the attic window at the three creaking farm carts that were bearing all that was left of the Culvers' possessions out of Widford Manor. There were few enough of them, and in poor condition, but they were dear to him, for they were old friends. There, sticking up out of the last cart, was a corner of the old, highly-carved battels chest, out of which he had taken many a crumb of manchet and sip of ale in the old days. The cart had stopped while the one in front of it was negotiating the ford, and Dick had half a mind to dodge down by the hedge, scramble into the cart and slip between the open bars of the chest before running water parted them. The Culvers had been good friends to him, and he would have liked to share their fortunes a little longer, especially as Nicholas Culver, the heir, was only ten years old: Dick had always liked children. But he had been at Widford time out of mind and had only known the Culvers for a little over two centuries; he would stay with the old place a little longer, and give it a chance of life; it would soon fall into ruin if he left it.

He came down from the attic and wandered over the deserted house. There was no need for caution now, and he whistled to himself with a high, soft, droning sound as he pattered over the dusty floors. The place had been dreary enough lately, since that wretched day of the sale, when Dick had lain under the joists of the roof to escape the clatter and trampling as the tapestries were pulled down, and the pictures taken off the walls, and men in ugly clothes dug about under the apple trees for the silver. Dick knew where that had been hidden, and he was pleased to see that the strangers had not found it. If they had got near the place he might have raised a storm to frighten them, or an alarm of fire; but he was dispirited these days, with no heart to play tricks on intruders, however much he disliked them. Since the sale old Peacock had lived on in the house, with narrow means, and among the poor sticks of furniture which had not been good enough to sell. Dick had no doubt when he took them away that he was going to Madam Culver and young Nicholas and the girl children, wherever they might be, and he was half inclined to give him a hint of where the silver was hidden; but he thought Master Richard might come back for it – it was he that had entrusted it to him – and he had the treasure-guarding instincts of his kind.

Dick missed old Peacock. He was slow, and deaf, and blind, but he was human company, and hobs fare ill without it. He went down to the kitchen, where he had often sat lately in the shadows, while Peacock drooped over the fire. There was an empty barrel there and some straw, a legged pot with one foot bent and some broken pipkins. An old broom stood behind the door, nearly bare of twigs, and Dick started to sweep up the straw and dust from force of habit; but there was no fire to burn it in and he soon propped up the broom again and drifted out into the yard. It seemed even emptier than the house. The deep, spring mud was trampled about and ploughed into ruts where the carts had been, but the cattle sheds and stables had long been empty, old Peacock's goat had gone with him, and the neighbours had carried away the hens in bunches, tied by the legs. The very cats had left them for the neighbouring farms. In the pale, spring sunshine the place looked hollow. Dick did not remember it so desolate for three hundred years.

A sudden clamour fell on the air, and a red hen, shouting her own praises, burst out from among the nettles. She had been laying out, and had escaped the round-up of the others. Dick was suddenly cheered. He felt too that an egg would make him a pleasant meal. The granary had long been empty, but he scrabbled up a few grains of wheat and carried them out to the hen. He called to her, and she came up readily enough to take the meal. The hens were sometimes nervous of him, and made a great cackling when he ran among them, but perhaps this one was lonely like him, for she let him tickle and preen her feathers with his thin, cold fingers.

'Ha, my Hicketty Picketty,' he said, 'you shall be my hen, my little red hen. I will find 'ee worms, and no fox shall touch you.'

The hen scrabbled and scratched about the yard, and Dick went lightly over to her nest among the nettles, and picked out the egg she had just laid from the ten hidden there. The hen scratched about without noticing him; indeed she was so stupid that he might have eaten her egg in front of her, and she would never have associated his meal with her family; but he felt that this would be ill-mannered, and he turned into the stable, and climbed on to the manger where

9

he often used to sit in old days. A shaft of sunshine warmed him there, and he bit the top off the egg and sucked it, and crumbled the shell into powder. He did not exactly need to eat, but an occasional meal was a pleasure to him, and he needed some comfort just then. Then, for he was a just hob, he picked up a piece of broken stick, and went into the garden to dig worms for his hen.

As days and weeks passed the loneliness about Widford deepened. If it had not been for Hobberdy Dick the house would have fallen into disrepair. He shut the attic windows when it rained, and opened them on sunny days to keep the house dry, and thrust back a stone slate that was loose on the roof. But the loneliness set him to seek for his own kind. In an ordinary way humans and domestic animals sufficed him for company; but he was a sociable creature, and one red hen, and that a stupid one, was not enough, and Widford Manor was ill supplied with hauntings. The shadowy Grim in the ruined chapel had grown more attenuated as years went by; and a hundred years ago had faded to no more than a voice. There was a dim ghost that frightened him in the west attic. It looked like a child who had died there two hundred years before, but the spirit informing it was of the child's stepmother, a woman whom Hobberdy Dick had always hated. He never went into that room if he could help it. There was an abbey lubber in Swinbrook Manor, just across the fields; but since the Reformation he had been a morose creature, dedicated to the destruction of the house he inhabited; he was no company for Dick. Half a mile downstream, just below Swinbrook, Long George, a hob who worked in a farm across the Windrush, used to dangle his legs in the water on warm nights, and Dick fell into the way of going down to play the echo game and ducks and drakes with him across the stream; but they were on opposite sides of the river, and neither cared to cross running water without a strong reason for it, so they were distant company for each other. On May Eve Dick was driven by loneliness to make the dangerous journey to the Rollright Stones in the hope of finding old friends at the May revels there. The journey was one of special danger in 1652, for black creatures were abroad at that time. It was not the human ghosts whom Dick feared, though they were many and restless just then, but the bogles and black spirits raised up by witchcraft. The witch trials had stirred up much mud lately, and the bogles and devils rose out of it like shrimps in a pond. At St John's Eve or All Hallows Dick would not have ventured; but May Eve was a merrier time, and he took his courage in his hands and went.

It was a long way over the hill to the Rollright Stones, but Dick's thin legs covered the ground quickly, and he was there before a human would have got a quarter of the way. It was a moonlight night, and Wychwood on that night was generally alive with human company, song and laughter and love talk. But this year Dick only saw a little band of children, sleepy and quiet, straggling about in search of wood anemones and flowering may. He climbed a tree and bent a branch so that they could reach it; then slipped away unseen, and skirted the gipsy encampment where a gay, ragged circle was singing to the moon with great leaps and wild dances. He struck some long ploughed strips beyond the forest, and then open upland, till he came in sight of the peering King of the stones, labouring up the hill for a sight of Long Compton.

It was a little time since he had been to the May Eve festivities at Rollright, and he had expected to find the stones in a glimmering circle of light. It was a disappointment to him to see the few, feeble Will o' the Wisps that bobbed about among them.

'Where be all the world?' he said aloud. 'It be a fair caddle, so it be, if this is all we can muster on May Eve.'

'Who'm that?' said a voice from among the shadows. 'Why 'tis Hobberdy Dick! Young Hobberdy Dick of Widford! 'Tis a long acorn-sprouting since I've had a tell with thee. Us thought thou wert laid this twenty May Days back.'

'I'm main pleased to see ye, Grim,' said Dick, greeting with some respect a venerable hobgoblin from Stow churchyard. ''Twill be long afore the acorn's rooted that cradles the man that'll lay me. Sometimes I wish 'twould come sooner. These be cruel hard times. I never thought to see so few here on May Eve; but 'tis black times for stirring abroad now.'

'Us never thought the like would happen again,' said Grim. 'Since the old days when the men in white came, and built the new church and turned I out into the cold yard I've never seen its like for strange doings. First I thought old days had come again; for they led the horses into the church in broad day; but the next day they led 'em out again. They'd just foddered 'em down for the night. And then they broke the masonry, and smashed up the brave windows of frozen air. And two years before they tore down the summer halls in my yard, and these ten years there's not been so much as a hobby-horse nor a dancer in the town.'

The Taynton Lob joined them – a small, good-natured creature with prick ears and hair like a mole's fur on his bullet head.

'It may be quiet in Stow,' he said, 'but there's more going on than I like in Taynton churchyard.'

'What sort?' said Hobberdy Dick.

'Women,' said the Lob half evasively, 'and the things that feed on 'em, and counter-ways pacing, and blacknesses.'

'There's always been that,' said the Church Grim, 'for so long as I can call to mind. That mixed up with t'other.'

'The t'other's gone, though,' said Lob, 'and that be all that's left. The trouble with we,' he went on sadly, 'is that we're neither one thing nor t'other. We're frittened of their holy water and the great things that come around them when they pray, but we're main frittened of their black bugs, and their counter-pacings and the deathly things they say. And it seems there's no place now for the likes of we.'

There was a murmur of assent from a small cluster of hobgoblins round them, which was broken by a high, thin laugh from the other side of the circle; and the cold air which followed the sound drove the hobgoblins into a tighter bunch. The wandering Will o' the Wisps which had been straying dispersedly among the stones drew together and moved towards the hobgoblins, who were on the south side of the circle, but the north side was not therefore dark; it began to shine with the blurred radiance of touchwood and corpse lights. From among the stones slipped queer, plasmic, shapeless forms, not unlike distorted shadows of the hobgoblins themselves, and the more dreadful to them for that. In ordinary times they would have trusted to their simple counter-charms and stood firm, but few, dispirited and war-weary as they now were, they drew back from the circle, and the corpse lights grew from a crescent to a horse-shoe, and then closed into a ring. The thin laughter rose higher, and was answered from the sky by a distant droning sound, the whiffle of wind through the dry twigs of broomsticks. The whole air

hummed with the sound, so that panic came upon the little bunch of good fellows, and they broke and ran helter-skelter in twos and threes. It was well for them that the things in the circle were waiting to greet the broomsticks, or they would have had little chance of escape.

Dick was giving an arm as he ran to the old Stow Church Grim, whom the Taynton Lob was supporting upon the other side. Old Grim whimpered as he ran, with small whines of distress, like a dog in a nightmare. He sometimes appeared in the form of a black dog, and unkind gossip had it that he always reverted to that shape if he stopped concentrating. However gossip seemed, as usual, to be mistaken, for now, when four legs would have served him well, he was still hobbling on his two thin shanks. When they came to a small stream flowing into one of the Wychwood meres they stopped to rest.

'There now,' said the Lob, ''tis southward flowing water, and there's not one of the three of us but can cross it if need be with no more nor a twinge; while as for the likes of they, 'tis death and vanishment for them to set so much as a whisker across it. So set 'ee down, Master Grim, and take your breath.'

Grim sat down, moaning, and rocking himself backwards and forwards.

'To think of it!' he said. 'To think of Old Grim turning tail to the likes of they after all that has come and gone! They may as well put old Grim in a bottle, and throw 'un in the Red Sea for any good there is in 'un.'

'Don't say that, Master Grim,' said Dick. ''Tis but for the moment. You'll daunten them again many's the time when better days come. Even now 'tis more than they dare do to front 'ee in Stow churchyard. 'Tis the kindly blood shed these ten years that makes 'em so bold. Come four years or five, when the green Earth's swallowed it, you'll see they'll be running back to their holes again.'

Old Grim seemed hardly to hear his words of consolation, but rocked himself and moaned as before.

'Us can't leave him to find his lonesome way to Stow,' said the Taynton Lob, 'so lost and wandered as he be. Lend us a hand, Dick, till we set he on his own mould.'

Hobberdy Dick was not one to refuse such a request; and they set out on the long, tedious tramp to Stow, with the whimpering and abstracted Grim between them. It was a walk not without some alarms. Once or twice they took shelter under a friendly elder tree at the sound of whickering over their heads; but they did not leave Grim until he was under the comfortable shelter of a fine ancestral tomb in Stow churchyard. Here he began to be more cheerful and collected and they left him without misgiving.

'He'm breaking up fast, be poor old Grim,' said the Taynton Lob. 'See us home to Taynton, Dick; 'tain't that far out of thy way.'

It added several miles to the walk, but Dick was too good-natured to refuse, and they went on sociably together, though not without precaution. It was clear dawn by now, and they were no longer afraid of bogles or warlocks, but they preferred to avoid the human company that was abroad. They went by ditch and hedgerow, talking together in their low, twittering voices, pitched rather for crickets than for human ears. At Taynton they parted reluctantly, and Dick dodged back by the hedges in broad daylight, and arrived home spent and leg-weary. The red hen ran out to meet him, and Dick was glad to refresh himself with a newly laid egg.

After his breakfast he sat in the sun, half dozing, and preening the shiny feathers on his hen's red neck.

'Eh, Hicketty Picketty,' he said. 'Widford's best, though it be empty-like. 'Tis a wicked world outside Widford these days, my little red hen.'

Two

A Master of a house (as I have read)
Must be the first man up, and last in bed:
With the Sun rising he must walk his grounds;
See this, view that, and all the other bounds:
Shut every gate; mend every hedge that's torne,
Either with old, or plant therein new thorne:
Tread ore his gleab, but with such care, that where
He sets his foot, he leaves rich compost there.

HERRICK

FROM May Day till Midsummer Hobberdy Dick
stayed close at Widford. The place was quiet and
empty. He never saw now the glint of the sun on steel
morions across the river, nor heard the pulse of scam-
pering hoofs that told of flight, nor the shouts of
pursuit. Sometimes neighbours came about the place to
fetch away planks and tools, and at the end of June
some boys climbed over the wall to pick the dwindling
strawberries. Dick would have welcomed their company, but every instinct of duty led him to guard the
place from theft. He climbed down into the draw-well,
and cried hollowly from it when neighbours came to
find pickings in the yard, and he droned and squealed
from the ivy when the boys browsed over the garden.
When some poachers climbed up to take lead from the
roof for their bullets he rose up like a great white owl
and all but knocked them from the ladder. His zeal
gave the place a bad name, so that it stood empty longer
than need be; indeed it was not until the beginning of
August that Dick saw a purchaser. He was sitting on
the roof in the sun, idly catching gnats and throwing

them to the weakling of a family of swallows – whose
flight was still staggering and uncertain, so that its
nimbler brothers snatched flies from under its beak –
when he saw three sturdy cobs turn the corner towards
the river and splash through the ford. He flattened
himself against the roof and peered over. Three riders
came up the lane to the Manor. The first Dick knew
by sight, he was a Bartholomew from Burford, who
had been about the house once or twice. The two who
followed him were strangers, and looked ill at ease on
horseback. One was old and the other young, but they
were of the same kind, and a kind unfamiliar to Hobberdy Dick. They rode their horses stiffly and seemed
glad to dismount from them, they wore dark, smooth
clothes, and their voices were high and clipped. The
younger may have been about seventeen, and he spoke
little – Dick took him to be the son of the elder one,
for though they were different in build and colouring
their features were something alike. They led the
horses into the stable and went into the house. Dick
slipped down a chimney and followed them from room
to room. They went through the house thoroughly,
the elder telling the boy to pace the rooms, and noting
down the measurements on a set of tablets. He stamped
on the floors to satisfy himself of the soundness of the
timbers, and felt the walls for damp. They peered into
the cupboards and went up into the attics and meas-
ured the width of the stairs until Dick was tired of
following them. He went down into the stables to see
what he could pick up from the horses, two of whom he
found uncomfortably hitched, so that they could hardly
eat the hay that had been left for them in the manger.
He slackened their headstalls and rubbed them down
with a wisp of hay. He gathered from their manner
that they were local horses, who did not know their

present riders, nor wish to extend their acquaintance. As he was finishing the last horse the boy came in to fetch food from the saddle bags. He patted the horses kindly but unhandily. Dick examined him through the slats of an empty manger. He was pale, like his father, with the same jutting-out, roughly chiselled nose, but his father was paunchy and he was thin, and his father's hair was dark brown, while his was almost colourless, and as fine and straight and shining as floss silk. His eyes were so light as to be almost yellow, and unevenly flecked with brown, so that one looked darker than the other. Dick's heart warmed to him, for he looked like a wild thing caged.

Three quarters of an hour later they came out of the house again, and round to the stables.

'Well, Mr Bartholomew,' the elder stranger was saying, 'if you will bid so far for me at the auction I shall be obliged. My wife is strongly inclined towards the place; the name seems a leading of Providence.'

'Yes, Widdison and Widford seem to belong to each other,' said Ned Bartholomew. 'Will you come back to Burford and drink a stirrup cup to the success of the deal?'

'Nay, I thank you, but we are later on our way to Oxford than I had reckoned. We will take the straight road. Good day to you. I hope we may meet again before long. Come, Joel.'

He mounted with some difficulty, and they rode off towards the ford, leaving Ned Bartholomew to lock up the house.

'Fat, pompous, city fool,' he said to his horse as he tightened his saddle girth, 'Widdison of Widford! I'll lay in ten years they'll say the place is named after them.'

He swung himself smartly into the saddle, and trotted off up the short cut to Fulbrook, where his father's new house looked south over the valley.

Dick heard no more for some time, and had almost forgotten the strangers when, almost a month later, the house was unlocked again, and women came with pails and brooms, and began to clean the floors and walls. Dick was rejoiced to see it, and where their cleaning came short of his standards he remedied it on the night-time, for they left their brooms behind them. Then wagons came creaking through the ford, carrying strange furniture, smelling of faraway places, which grazed the walls as it was carried in. An old woman came with it, who scolded and ordered the men about in a high, screaming voice. Dick did not think he would like her, but she would not be alone in the house, if the furniture was any warrant. More was carried in than Dick remembered to have seen in the Culvers' richest days. There were carved bedsteads for the first-floor rooms, and truckle beds to go under them, and pallet beds for the attics, and more beds in the closets below stairs. There were tables and carved chairs, and stools, and battels chests and armoires. There was an embroidery frame and a spinning wheel, and a harpsichord. There was a carved wooden cradle too. Hobberdy Dick thought with a leaping heart that the house would be full again, and there would be children and merry days as there had been before.

At first the furniture was strange to the house, and he polished it and shifted it about a little, to make it feel at home. It was well cared for, but it smelt of soot and sea-coal. One bed gave him more trouble than anything else in the house, for it was haunted, and he wished they would take it to the west attic, so that the two ghosts might fight it out together; but it was a fine bed with embroidered hangings to it, and they put it in the best room. There the ghost counted his money bags, hour after hour. Dick could hear the clinking all night, while he was working about the place. It was a dull ghost and no company at all.

When the furniture was in, the house started being cleaned all over again. Mrs Biddums, the old woman with the shrill voice, did not sleep in the house. For all her fierce ways she was nervous, and glanced fearfully round the rooms when she was left alone. She slept in the mill across the ford until the rest of the family arrived.

They came after Michaelmas, in two covered wagons, with the two Widdisons riding beside. Dick, sitting in the nearest oak tree, for safety against strange dogs, watched them unpack themselves. There was the mistress of the house, more richly dressed than the men, and younger than her husband, and an old lady in black, quiet and tired. There were three little girls, the eldest about the age of Dick's favourite, Nicholas Culver, and a little boy in skirts, led by the second of them, and a baby carried by a young nurse. There was a middle-aged manservant and a half-grown boy, and three servant girls. With their packages and bundles, and jars of wine, and baskets of clothes they filled the two wagons to bursting. They unpacked themselves with great noise and clamour and argument – the high, harsh-pitched, city voices reminded Dick of a flock of starlings in debate. At last every bundle had been carried into the house, the horses were stabled, plumes of smoke went up from the chimneys, a good smell of food and a scraping of knives showed that the place was fully occupied at last. Dick went to feed his little red hen, whom he had hidden in the wood for safety until new hens arrived and he could smuggle her in among them. He promised her top pecking rights as she took the grain from his lean fingers.

That night Dick wandered through a well-filled house, and inspected the sleeping arrangements. Mr and Mrs Widdison slept in the best room in the haunted bedstead, Mr Widdison tossing uneasily and muttering of money ventures, Mrs Widdison sound asleep, and the ghost wedged uneasily between them. The little boy slept in the truckle bed, drawn out from under theirs. One room on this floor was empty for a spare room, and in another the three little girls slept, with the baby and its nurse. The old lady slept in a small closet room, and Joel in a recess under the stairs. The west attic was empty, and Mrs Biddums slept in the east attic. Between the two was the dormitory of the three maids. The manservant and the boy slept below stairs, and the two wagoners in a loft above the stables.

The wagoners went next day, taking the horses and wagons with them, but in a few days a cattleman came, who slept in the loft. He was a Burford man. Ned Bartholomew came over to advise about horses and cattle. It was clear that Mr Widdison intended to try his hand at farming, and Dick foresaw hard work for himself, for here was a master's foot that would fat no land. He felt himself lucky with the cattleman, who was cross-grained and surly enough, but one that knew the ways both of beasts and land, and would be a useful man if left to follow his own counsel. He knew enough too to leave out his portion for Dick, which the town-bred maids neglected to do, though there were pickings enough in the kitchen.

At the end of the week some three dozen hens arrived, and Dick introduced his own among them, taking care to give her a position of authority. Within a few days she was established with the chief pecking rights, though there were many more intelligent hens in the yard.

One of the maidservants, a girl of sixteen called Charity, was put in charge of the hens. She knew little about them, but she was pleased with the charge, and George Batchford, the cattleman, took a kindness for her, and gave her help and advice. She spent longer over her duties than Mrs Biddums approved, and was always being called into the house.

One evening as they were watching the hens feed she said to George Batchford:

'Seems to me there's one hen more always nor what we brought. Yon little red one is different from the rest.'

'One extra is there?' said George Batchford. ''Tis yon little red one, ye say?' He sank his voice low. 'Mind and give yon hen plenty to eat, and never lay a hand on her, whichever goes for the pot. If there's a beast more on a farm than ye can reckon for pay good heed to it. Ye never know who put it there.'

Charity looked up at him with large eyes.

'What do you mean, Mr Batchford?' she whispered. 'Not the fairies?'

'Name no names,' said George Batchford. 'There's some makes good neighbours if they're treated right, and Widford is well known to be a lucky place and well guided. Least said soonest mended, but give an extra handful to yon little red hen, and the poultry will prosper with you.'

'Charity! Charity! Where's that hoyt?' called Mrs Biddums from the back door. 'Does it take you an hour to throw a bowl of meal to the poultry? There's all to be done inside. There's the pots to be scoured, and the children's suppers to take up, and the mistress's face-

24

cream to skim and pot, and the scullery floor to scrub. Where's the eggs for the syllabub?'

'Seems to me all that's done in this house has to be done by Charity,' said George Batchford as she ran in. 'They'd be in a pretty caddle without her, to judge by the screams that old pea-hen does let out.'

It was late in the year to buy much in the way of cattle. A week later one cow in milk arrived, and a few bullocks for the winter. George Batchford was sent to buy a few pigs from Burford, and a couple of stout horses were bought, to work on the farm and pull Mrs Widdison's coach. The coach arrived soon after them from a coachmaker in Oxford, bright with its black and yellow paint, with a gay coat of arms painted on its panel. By this time Mrs Widdison had her house in order, and sat in her well-hung parlour every morning, waiting for visitors to come. Few came.

The youngsters of the family were those whom Dick watched most assiduously. They were as strange to him as their elders. At first they seemed frightened of everything. They cried and retreated if the cock came toward them, called the cow a bull, and were equally afraid of the horses' heads and hoofs. They were afraid to leave the path for thorns and nettles, and their clothes seemed their first care. Dick would have been ready to give them up if it had not been for the little boy, who came tottering after the cattleman, impeded by his long skirts, falling into the pig swill and under the horses' hoofs, and chattering incoherently all the time. Martha, the second girl, generally came after him, daring the poultry and the bullocks for his sake; and her courage soon earned its reward, and she ceased to be frightened. She was a sturdy, brown-eyed child of eight; and within a few weeks the creatures who had been so dreadful to her became her chief friends.

She seemed to be Joel's favourite, and he first brought her to feed the farm horses with bread, and set her up one day on his pony, and ran beside her up and down the field, till her mother tapped on the parlour window, and screamed for her to be taken down and sent into the house. Dick still liked his first friend, Joel, the best. He alone of them, from the beginning, seemed to be in an ecstasy with the country. Early in the morning, before sunrise, while Dick was lying curled in front of the kitchen embers, he would come tiptoeing downstairs with his shoes in his hands, unlatch a window and slip out. Dick sometimes followed him on his expeditions, which were not, like a country boy's, for fishing or sport, but mere rambling and entranced wanderings, to look and listen and smell. Sometimes he knelt down, and then Dick stood aloof, fascinated and terrified; sometimes he laughed and hummed to himself, and crashed merrily through the woods; and then Dick rustled along beside him companionably. Once, when they were both unawares, he caught a moment's glimpse of Dick, and stopped, startled and almost frightened; but Dick rallied all his powers, and thought of a clump of ferns with a rabbit peering out of it until he looked like one, and Joel went on, reassured. Before the family met for morning prayers Joel would be back, with his soft hair sleeked down, and only his wet feet to betray his early rambles. But his pale, fair skin began to be faintly bronzed.

Another person of the household who seemed pleased with the country was the old lady, Mrs Dimbleby. There was a little arbour in the walled garden where she would sit for hours on end in the cold sunshine, mending or knitting, or hearing the children their lessons, or with a Bible before her. Dick was rather frightened of her because of a luminous cloud in which she often sat; but he was fascinated, and she looked so mild and quiet that he could not think her dangerous. Joel came to talk to her there sometimes, and tell her what was done on the farm, and of country sports he had watched, and sometimes been asked to join. He had begun to help George about the place, and soon began to know some of the Burford boys.

One sunny day towards the end of October Dick wakened from a doze in the pile of dead leaves and garden rubbish at the back of the arbour to hear Joel talking angrily.

'Isn't it too bad, Gran, that I, who like it best, should be the one to leave it? The others wouldn't care if they never saw Widford again; but I'm the one that's to go back to Cheapside, among the noise and the smells, and yell "What d'ye lack!" in a booth. I've never done more than my formal apprenticeship because of my schooling, and I'm too young to be a merchant. My father's men will make nothing of me, and think me only sent up to bear tales. And indeed what else can I do? I've no authority with them.'

'It's hard, my dear,' said Mrs Dimbleby. 'I've seen what the country life means to you. Country blood will out, and your mother was fretting sorely for the country when you were born. But you have a first duty to your father, and if you obey it cheerfully it will turn to good in the end.'

'But my father never meant such a thing at first!' said Joel. 'I was to stay here, and perhaps have a tutor and go to College, if I was not too old and slow. He said as much to me when we rode down here together. It's all Mrs Widdison, who is angry because I have been asked here and there, while she sits in her fine parlour and waits for company to come. She'd be pleased enough to be in with the lot who've asked me over to

Shipton if she could. We'd hear nothing then of idle ways and ill companions. She's been a real stepmother to me since little Samuel was born.'

'Stepmother is not a kind nor a pleasant word for my Joel to use,' said Mrs Dimbleby. 'My girl would never have grudged a second wife to her husband, to cheer him and care for him after she was gone. And you've got her sweet nature, my dear, and would never grudge nor take it unkindly that your little half-brother should have his share of love. It hurts my very heart to see your poor mother-in-law so disappointed. She was set like a child on her fine plans; but country folk take a while to turn things over in their minds, and the gentlefolk, who follow the King, will not care to notice them that have bought their land from the Parliament; and the graver kind, I daresay, have no use for visiting nor gaieties. So day after day that poor young thing sits there like a child expecting a new toy that never comes. Small wonder if she is fretful sometimes. You must have patience and think kindly of her.'

The words dropped softly and slowly from the old lady, like the bemusing notes of a bird's evening song, seeming rather to belong to the silence than to break it. Her voice had a country lilt, though it was not the intonation that Dick knew, and he drew near and listened with pleasure. Joel's ill humour seemed to melt at the sound; and even after she had ceased he sat by her in silence.

'Well, I'll try to be good, Gran,' he said at length. 'Though it seems as if I was made for this place.'

'The Lord will bless your obedience to you, my dear,' said his grandmother, 'and sweeten the bread of duty. Go in and show yourself happy to obey him.'

'I'd better go now,' said Joel, 'and get it over. I came out before my father had time to tell me.'

He went into the house. Hobberdy Dick left the garden, and went into the stable yard to consider. He did not want them to send Joel away from the place, but he could think of no way to induce them to keep him.

Three

Thus many trickes I, Pach, can doe;
But to the good I ne'er was foe:
The bad I hate and will doe ever,
Till they from ill themselves doe sever:
To help the good Ile run and goe:
The bad no good from me shall know.

The Life of Robin Goodfellow

TEN days were to elapse before Joel went, and Dick
set to work to give him a reputation for competence
about the farm. There was all to be done about the
neglected place, and few to do it. Joel was willing and
helpful, though so ignorant and unhandy that Dick
and George Batchford must laugh at the way he set to
work; yet Dick saw to it that whatever he set his hand
to prospered. There was no crop to lift but darnels and
thistles, so they ploughed the neglected fields early.
The steady horses started aside from George's practised
hand, but they went straight for Joel – Dick led them.
When they fenced the gaps in the hedge Joel's work
continued in his absence, when they picked the apples
his basket was full first. Sometimes the cow even held
back her milk and would only let it down for Joel.
Once when Charity was busy Joel gathered the eggs,
and some which Dick had secreted the day before went
into his basket. It was clear to George Batchford that
it would be ruination to the place to let Joel go, but
Dick's trouble was that the master was so ignorant that
he noticed nothing. George felt the same, but he at
least could speak to Mr Widdison, and being a con-

scientious man, with the good of the stock at heart, he tried to do so.

On the Saturday before Joel was to leave, when Batchford went in with his tallies, he said, 'The young master shapes well to the work of the place.'

'I have no intention for him to work here,' said Mr Widdison. 'He goes back to London on Tuesday.'

'You'll not find things go so well here when the young master's away,' said George Batchford. 'There's all to do about the place, and we'm cruel short-handed. I'll not say the young master's knowledgeable, but he'm lucky. He've green fingers, and the place will fare well while he's about it.'

'I did not buy this place that my son should serve as a day-labourer under the cattleman,' said Mr Widdison. 'Mr Bartholomew told me you were a good man at your work, but if you can't do without the help of a boy like my son, who's never worked in the country in his life, I shall think the worse of you.'

'It's not his help I'm wanting,' said George Batchford, 'though the Lord knows there's enough to be done here, and few enough to do it. Can't you understand a simple thing, Master? I tell you, the lad's green-fingered, and we'll fare to do ill if he goes.'

'I don't know what you're talking of. It sounds to me a piece of heathen nonsense. When I want your advice I'll ask it.'

'You'll not get it,' said George Batchford. ''Tis a true saying that he who sows words reaps naught but chaff.' He went muttering out of the house and into the stable. 'There's no fool like an old fool, 'tis true enough. Don't you hold it against me if he goes,' he said to the silence. 'I tried my best to keep the lad, knowing as you have a fancy for him; but the old fool can't see reason when 'tis set straight in front of he.

Don't take it out of me, nor the cattle, for 'tain't none of our fault.'

Hobberdy Dick heard the plea, for he was sitting on one of the rafters, eating a piece of wheaten cake, which he had taken from the kitchen. Annoyed as he was at the ill success of his plans he realized the justice of what Batchford said, and let drop a piece of cake beside him as a token of good will. Batchford started back, and raised a white, frightened face to the roof, but saw nothing, for Dick was lying flat along his rafter. He picked up the piece of cake and examined it. At last he said, 'Thank 'ee kindly,' in a low voice, and ate it up. George Batchford, Dick noted with approval, knew what was what.

Tuesday came, and Joel rode off to Burford, where he was to meet some wool merchants travelling back to London, and get their convoy through the highwaymen and broken men who lurked on the outskirts of the city. His little sisters waved scarves after him, and Hobberdy Dick sat up in his oak tree and watched him out of sight. Then he climbed down the tree and set himself to do some discriminating mischief. The trouble was that the blame would so often be put on the wrong person. He did not want to touch George Batchford or the cattle; and indeed the whole farm was Batchford's province, where it would be easier to prove that Joel was needed. A personal lesson to Mr Widdison seemed the only thing, but Dick was afraid that he would learn slowly. He went into the garden and collected all the spiders he could find, several hundred of them, and put them into the Widdison's bedroom. It was Mrs Widdison who minded them most.

After that the best bedroom was a lively place. Dick sprang the mousetraps and loosed the mice there. He caught the rats that were lurking round the poultry, and carried them upstairs. This served a double purpose, it protected his own red hen and it annoyed the Widdison's. When the rats and mice were not scrabbling and scuttering in the wainscot he imitated them. Sometimes he hooted like a screech-owl, or meowled like a cat trapped behind the wainscot. Even the ghost glanced up sometimes from its money bags, and Mrs Widdison was terrified. She said it was more than mortal rats or mice, which was true enough, and that the house was haunted, and that if she had known it would be like that in the country she would have stayed in Cheapside.

This talk checked Dick a little. It would be like the foolish woman to take them all back to town, and he did not want the house left empty. Something must be done to make the place attractive to her. In the meantime he destroyed the roots of the gooseberry bushes and blew canker on to the roses. If he could get some of the neighbours to visit, he thought, it would tie the woman to the place. It was some weeks before he had an opportunity to direct fortune, and in the interval he led little Samuel into mischief.

At last, one November afternoon, he saw the Fettiplace coach lumbering majestically along on the other side of the Windrush, on its way to Burford. The running water was between them, and Dick plunged into it. The cold stream felt like death, stabbing quivers of pain ran up him, but he struggled bravely through, and met the coach. It was drawn by four horses, a somewhat mixed team, since even the great wealth of the Fettiplaces had been affected by the War. He swarmed up the leader of the team, gripped his mane firmly, and turned his head towards the ford. The horse reared and trembled with terror, and the rest were infected with his panic. The boy riding the leader felt a cold presence in front of him, gave a yell of terror, and flung himself off. There was a cry from one of the ladies inside, and a bubbling scream from the maid. The coach rocked and jolted madly as it was dragged into the stream. Dick clapped his hand over his mouth to keep from a loud ho! ho! ho! that would betray him. The horses panted and struggled to get free from their harness and plunge apart, the coach lurched up out of the stream, and there was a tearing crack as the shaft broke. Most of the inhabitants of Widford had hurried out. George Batchford ran to the horses' heads, Dick slipped down and began to soothe his mount, the coach tottered and heeled over on its side.

Mrs Widdison came to the coach door. Old Madam Fettiplace, silent and still stately, though stout, was helped out; her gentle daughter-in-law, who had received her weight when the coach overturned, was winded and almost unconscious, the maid was in strong hysterics.

'Oh Madam!' said Mrs Widdison. 'What a terrible thing! And what a Providence that no greater harm was done! Pray come in and rest yourself and take some refreshment.'

She helped her, still silent, into the house, and sent Ursula for arnica and hot water, and the men for wine and cakes. 'We are but half settled in here,' she said. 'I am waiting to find a gentlewoman who suits me, so I fear we cannot give the attendance we could wish.'

Mrs Dimbleby was helping young Lady Fettiplace into a chair, and bathing a bruised temple with arnica. Rachel, the eldest child, was holding the basin for her, and looking with awed eyes past them to old Madam Fettiplace, installed in the best chair. Martha had coaxed the maid into the kitchen, and Samuel was watching George Batchford and the shamefaced postilion as they examined the horses. Dick peered into the window, and marked the bustle, and Mrs Widdison's awed and enraptured face with a happy grin. 'He'll not shift her this side of Christmas,' he thought, well satisfied.

'Well,' said Madam Fettiplace at length, 'it hardly looks as if we'll get to the Dower House tonight. A curse on all coaches, say I! New-fangled, racketty contrivances! If we'd been riding pillion or in a sensible horse litter this would never have happened. Will you send your good man out to see what's amiss, and if the horses have hurt themselves. I don't know what ailed them to make for the ford like that. It is years since they have taken that way.'

Mr Widdison, who was bowing in the doorway, turned hastily to go on the errand, but his wife had more spirit. 'One of the men shall go,' she said. 'We want you to persuade Madam Fettiplace to remain here tonight. It is not fit she should move after the great shock and danger she has been in.'

'Tilly vally!' said the old lady. 'If we are not able to go on to Burford we can go back half a mile across the fields. I'll send that silly lad back for my pony.'

'Oh Madam, for that matter you can have our coach. But there is no hurry. You will at least stay to a foolish, trifling little repast, just what we have in the house, and forgive the want of ceremony. Mr Widdison, do you stay with my lady, and I will give orders to have it got ready.'

She hurried out of the room, drawing Rachel with her. Madam Fettiplace would have refused curtly enough, but when she called Lady Fettiplace to come with her Mrs Dimbleby said in her soft, calm voice, 'I fear there is some injury here. There may be a rib broken. It would be wiser for my lady to rest a little.'

'Really, Anne,' said Madam Fettiplace in some annoyance, 'you might have chosen another place to break your ribs. Young people seem to be made of glass nowadays. They break if you look at them.'

Dick thought with a chuckle that, severe as Madam Fettiplace's looks were, they could hardly compete with her thirteen stone of weight when it came to breaking bones. Lady Fettiplace flushed.

'It won't hurt me to move,' she said; but when she tried to get up her colour faded, and Mrs Dimbleby said; 'You had better stay here, my lady; we will help you to bed and give you something warm to drink, and in the morning you will be better able to move. We will send over to your lord and tell him there is no great thing amiss with you. Come, Samuel, we will put my lady in the arm chair, and the men shall carry her upstairs.'

For the moment, it seemed, Madam Fettiplace had nothing to say, and before she could interpose Mrs Dimbleby's swift gentleness had carried her point. Lady Fettiplace was carried upstairs, and in a few minutes Mrs Widdison came back to conduct Madam Fettiplace to a room where she could wash and have her clothes put to rights. All that the resources of the house could do at such short notice was done to make the meal as magnificent as possible. There was fine sugar and foreign conserves in the store room – more than even the larger country houses could boast – and with its embroidered linen and silver goblets the table made a rich showing; but all was done with a good deal of bustle. Mrs Dimbleby, who alone did things quickly and quietly, was in attendance on Lady Fettiplace, Mrs Biddums could be heard scolding shrilly in the distance, and Mr and Mrs Widdison were full of officious attentions.

They were bestowed on an unresponsive object. Madam Fettiplace sat upright and forbidding in her chair, almost silent. She ate with a good appetite indeed, but she praised nothing, and gave only the barest and most formal thanks. While the meal was going on the best bedroom was being cleaned, the sheets were hurriedly stripped off the best bed and the best embroidered ones were put on it. Mrs Widdison might have spared herself the trouble of putting them out, for Madam Fettiplace did not mean to stay. Before the meal was over a groom had arrived with a lantern and a pillion behind his saddle and in a quarter of an hour the bed was being re-made, as he rode back across the rimey November fields with Madam Fettiplace behind him.

In spite of this Mrs Widdison went to bed in high spirits.

'You may say what you like, Samuel,' she said, 'and the old lady can be as stiff as she likes, but once my Lady Fettiplace has spent a night in the house they will be bound to show us some attention.'

'And what good will it do us?' said Samuel Widdison. 'That's what I look to. If the godly men in the place hear that we are in with the cavalier families it will go against us. And I've all but been asked to join the Sequestration Committee. That's where our interest lies.'

'Tush!' said his wife. 'That class of people are of no weight at all. The old cavalier families are the gentry, and always will be. They are the people to know.'

'You're old-fashioned in your ideas, my mouse. The day of these people has gone past. What's this old Madam Fettiplace to give herself such airs? Her husband hanging round the exiled court, her brother-in-law mumping about with a broken heart, her son

37

boggling and pleading with sequestration committees in half a dozen counties! The Fettiplaces may be rich enough at present, but it won't last. The people to be in with are the godly men of good standing. They're coming up in the world and the others are coming down.'

'You were ready enough to be civil to them today.'

'A man must be civil in his own house, and besides I am in the way of treating them with respect in the course of business. I bear them no ill will, mind you, though I don't hold with their principles. Indeed in the way of business I'd rather deal with them than the others, for they know a good thing when they see it, and are above huckstering and beating a man down. Still, they're a godless lot, and the hand of the Lord is heavy on them. Those that cleave to them will go down with them.'

For all that Lady Fettiplace was treated with assiduous attention the next morning. She might have remained many days in the house, and was indeed left over the Sunday. Then Sir John Fettiplace returned from Buckingham, and arrived with the second coach, ill pleased to find that his wife had been left to the chance treatment of strangers. He thanked the Widdisons more courteously than his mother had done, but with some distaste, and helped his wife solicitously into the coach, while the Widdisons bowed and curtsied at the door. As she went out Lady Fettiplace caught at old Mrs Dimbleby's hand.

'Thank you for your kindness,' she said hurriedly. 'Will you come and see me sometimes?'

'If ever you need me I will come,' said Mrs Dimbleby.

The next day a handsome present of game arrived for the Widdisons; but that was the last they heard from the Fettiplaces for some time. Mrs Widdison tried to inspirit her husband to ride over and inquire after Lady Fettiplace, but he would not go. The present of game had done him an ill turn already, for Mrs Widdison had boasted of it to John Sylvester, who had come to dinner in time to taste it, and Mr Widdison felt that his credit with the Puritan party had been lowered in consequence. His name was not on the Sequestration Committee, and he blamed the Fettiplace game for his exclusion.

Four

But well-a-day, the gardener careless grew;
The maids and fairies both were kept away,
And in a drought the caterpillars threw
Themselves upon the bud and every spray.
    God shield the stock! if heaven send no supplies,
    The fairest blossom of the garden dies.

W. BROWNE

SOME days later Mrs Dimbleby put on a warm cloak,
tied a kerchief firmly over her cap, and set out with
brisk, light steps across the wintry fields towards Swinbrook. Hobberdy Dick, who had fallen into a state
of indecision between his desire to keep Widford
tenanted and his determination to show them that Joel
was needed at home, was glad to see someone take
action, and went up to the roof to watch for her return.
It was falling dark as she came back, and he scrambled
down into the house, to see if he could learn anything
of her errand. As he came to the top of the stairs, however, his attention was deflected, for he saw Nicholas
Culver sliding down the bannisters, dressed in the
holland smock he used to wear when he played in the
garden. He landed lightly at the bottom, and brushed
past Mrs Dimbleby as she came into the house. Dick
ran down the dark stairs, and out after him into the
garden. Young Nick had gone along to the beehives,
and was leaning over one of them. So Hobberdy Dick
saw clearly enough from the corner of the house; but
when he got to the terrace where the hives stood no-one
was there, only from inside them came a significant,
whining, drowsy hum. Dick turned back uneasily into

40

the house, with a forgotten but familiar pain turning in him like a knife. He wandered, miserable and restless, about the place, and even stared morbidly into the west attic. He had no heart to try to find out about Mrs Dimbleby's errand. At supper time, however, he heard something of it. His hen had gone to roost long ago, and he was too wretched for solitude. Inferior as he felt the family to be to Nicholas Culver and all his ancestors, they were yet human company. He was sitting under the table, with an arm round the purring cat, when Mrs Widdison returned to her often-defeated purpose.

'Really, Samuel, I am quite uneasy about not hearing of poor Lady Fettiplace. I feel sure she must be still laid up, or she would have called to thank us for our attention. You know *I* can't go, but it would be quite fitting, as I'm tired of telling you, for you to go. Perhaps they are waiting for it.'

'And I'm tired of telling you that I see no reason for going,' said Mr Widdison. 'The less we see of those gentry the better for our welfare, in this world and the next.'

'You need not be anxious, Rachel,' said Mrs. Dimbleby, 'The young lady is better, though I do not think she will ever be robust.'

'How do you know, Mrs Dimbleby?'

'I went to see her this afternoon.'

'You went to see her? Why didn't you tell me? It is not fitting. Surely you didn't take the coach without asking me?'

'There was no need for the coach; I walked across the fields.'

'But you shouldn't have done that. You shouldn't walk like a serving woman across the fields. The Fettiplaces will look down upon us ever after. How did you get in? I'm sure Madam Fettiplace would never admit you.'

'On a sudden I felt a heat towards going, so I knew there would be no difficulty about being admitted. And she was glad of company, her husband is from home.'

Mrs Widdison tossed her head, and her silks and curls rustled. 'Upon my word!' she said; but at a look from her husband she bit her speech off short, and the old lady went on placidly eating her supper in silence.

After a long pause Mrs Widdison's curiosity got the better of her, and she said with a jerk: 'And what did you talk about?'

'Our talk followed our thoughts,' said Mrs Dimble-by, and volunteered no more.

Little Martha, sitting half asleep in her chair, broke off a crumb of manchet, and held it down to Hobberdy Dick, who was grateful for this human attention and took it from her warm, brown hand.

'Martha, how often have I told you not to crumble your food and throw it about?' said her mother sharply. 'Are you feeding the cat there under the table? I won't have it in the room.'

'Come, my mouse,' said Samuel, 'the cat does no harm, and keeps the mice from coming among the rushes. But you shouldn't throw good food about, Martha. A cat fed is a cat spoiled so far as mousing is concerned, and that is what cats are for.'

Martha said nothing, for she was doubtful what to say, and sleepy besides; and the brisk skirmish died away into silence. But Mrs Widdison did not forget her grievance. That night, as Dick wandered restlessly into the best bedroom, he heard her saying: 'Your Mother-in-law is deep, Samuel, you can't deny that: deep and sly. Did you mark how she slipped away from my question tonight?'

Mr Widdison said nothing and breathed deeply.

'It's no use your pretending to go to sleep, Samuel. There's no denying that the Fettiplaces have used us shockingly. If Mrs Dimbleby can demean herself to go creeping in among them it is more than I shall do. But they needn't think they can drive us away from here. I'll meet them in their own coin.'

'Better have no more to do with them,' said Mr Widdison. 'They've too much land and money and connections for us to cross them. But let them alone, and in one generation, or two, their pride will come down.'

'Yes, and our children's children will look down on theirs. I've found one way to pay them off, for so grand as they think themselves. I'll take that waiting maid we were talking of.'

'But you thought she was too young and slight and quiet in her ways for you.'

'No matter, I'll take her, and brisken her up. The old woman as good as said that she is a far-way cousin to the Fettiplaces. Old Madam would stare if she knew I had her cousin as a waiting woman. I'll hire her tomorrow.'

This conclusion seemed to give Mrs Widdison some satisfaction, and she turned over and settled herself to sleep.

Dick was on tiptoe next day when the coach went out, to see who this new waiting gentlewoman was to be. Unless Mrs Widdison had been gulled she came of the old families, and of neighbour blood. It seemed she was to sleep in the west attic. The maids were banging about there in a perfunctory way; no one cared to stay in that room long. It was a clear, fresh, watery day, with the last leaves spinning slowly down, and Dick

43

sat in his oak tree to watch for the coach's return. When at length it drew up at the door, and a small, slim figure followed Mrs Widdison out of it Dick nearly fell from his perch. By hempen and hampen it was no other than Anne Seckar! It was eight years since he had seen her, and she had been a small child then, but she had been the Culvers' favourite cousin, and she had guided young Nicholas Culver's first staggering steps when she had been no more than six years old. The time was when she had been the only child about the house. Here was someone indeed to whom Dick's heart could warm. Put her in the west attic! He'd turn the ghost out with his own hands, if need be. He climbed down his tree, and followed them into the house. Mrs Widdison was already mounting the stairs to her room, followed by Anne Seckar. She was all afire to display the richness of her plenishings, and left Anne no leisure to go to her own room, or take off her kerchief and hood. Anne set her little bundle down outside the door, and followed Mrs Widdison into the best room. Old Ursula Biddums was in attendance, sour and aggrieved at this newcomer to steal her mistress's favour. She opened cupboards and chests, while Mrs Widdison talked of care in pressing, washing and mending, and what could be re-made or fresh trimmed.

'Mind, I'll have no idle ways,' she said. 'No hanging and mooning about. There's always work to be done for a willing needle, and if you have finished here Mrs Biddums will find you plenty to do. Besides you will have to do the conserves and sweetmeats and pickles. And I will have no pickings and perquisities. I have heard of your fine, idle maids' ways. And if I find you wearing my ribbons and laces you'll have your gown pulled over your ears, and may out to the roads to beg your bread.'

Anne made no reply, but turned away to put back the gown she had been holding. Dick was furious. He slipped into the shadow of the dressing chest, shot out a long arm, and with his thin, sharp fingers pinched Mrs Widdison viciously in the leg. She gave a short scream, and clapped her hand to the place, but could find nothing to account for the pain. In his heart Dick promised her a good pinching that night as she slept. One pinch was less than she deserved, but at least it altered the current of her thought. She told Anne to take off her kerchief, and show what she could do in the way of hairdressing. Anne folded her kerchief and put it on her bundle outside the door. Mrs Biddums went down to see about the dinner, and Anne returned, with cold and shaking fingers, to do the best she could with Mrs Widdison's elaborate curls. Mrs Widdison was ill satisfied.

'I can see you have everything to learn,' she said. 'And you seem stupid besides. I hope the sewing you showed me was your own, or I have a poor bargain with you.'

By the time she began to be satisfied dinner was ready, and Anne went downstairs behind her to help with carving, and stand behind Mrs Widdison's chair, holding her fan and handkerchief. The children stared at the new gentlewoman who had made their mother into a fine lady, as grand as Madam Fettiplace at the Manor; Mrs Widdison talked in a high, drawling voice, of the gossip about General Cromwell's household and the parties at General Lambert's house. Mrs Dimbleby answered occasionally with a placid monosyllable. Mr Widdison grunted, or, what was worse still, interposed a tradesman's comments on the prices that had been paid, or such an one being in debt, the children stared silently. It was a conversation not to be sustained, and

45

presently Mrs Widdison called sharply for her pomander, and sent Anne running to look for it.

After dinner Mrs Widdison rose up, and said 'Come, Samuel, you must leave your pipe today. I want you in the Withdrawing Room to hear how my gentlewoman can sing and play. She is supposed to have some skill there, and I hope it will prove so.'

'Let Samuel smoke his pipe first, my dear,' said Mrs Dimbleby. 'He will be the better judge, and your little gentlewoman can have her snack and sup, and will play the better for it. It's ill setting to work in a strange place on an empty stomach.'

'That's right,' said Mr Widdison. 'It's not many comforts I stand for, but I must have my pipe of tobacco after dinner if I am to use a cool judgement.'

'Oh, very well, then,' said Mrs Widdison. 'You can eat there while they are clearing; but don't take all night over it.'

She called the servants to clear, and left the room, but Mrs Dimbleby poured out a glass of wine, put together the best of what was left, called Anne to sit, and sat down beside her.

'It is a novelty in the house to have a gentlewoman,' she said, 'and my daughter-in-law has yet to find how to fit you into our ways. Things will be easier in a day or two. Drink up your wine and take your bit at leisure. You are cold, and tired with the novelty of it all. I'll take you into the Withdrawing Room when you are done.'

Anne thanked her with a trembling voice, and sipped the wine and began to eat. Martha came up to the table to watch her.

'Is it true that you're a cousin of Madam Fettiplace?' she asked.

'Oh no,' said Anne. 'My great grandmother was a

47

Fettiplace, that's all. That's why the Fettiplace arms are carved there.'

'Is this your house, then?' said Martha.

'No, oh no. It's your father's house. Please don't say that.'

'That's enough, Martha,' said Mrs Dimbleby. 'Leave her in peace, and go and get out your sewing. Shall we go into the parlour now?' she said presently. 'We shall dearly love to hear your singing.'

Rachel and Martha went to fetch their samplers – embroidery for Rachel and plain mending stitches for Martha – and Mrs Dimbleby took Anne into the Long Parlour. Hobberdy Dick came out from under the table, and went to fetch a dish of cream and a piece of manchet from the larder and take them up to the west attic. Anne should not starve if he had any hand in the matter.

It was late, however, before Anne went up to her room. She had hastily washed herself and sleeked her hair, but she had had no time to find out where she was to sleep until Mrs Widdison was undressed, a process protracted that night until Mr Widdison began to grow impatient. Then at length she was free to pick up her bundle and follow Mrs Biddums up the stairs.

'Not the west attic?' she said, shrinking, as they reached the door.

'And what's the matter with it?' said Mrs Biddums. 'Too good for you, I should say. I see no sense in cockering up a young girl with a room to herself. Waiting gentlewoman here and waiting gentlewoman there! A plain maidservant was good enough for her in Cheapside, and why she should want better in this place, staring out over a dirty farmyard, beats me. Get in with you, and mind you're up betimes in the morning.'

Before she had finished Anne had opened the door resolutely, and shut it after her, with a murmured good night. Mrs Biddums picked her way among the sleeping maids to her own east attic. As she passed him Dick vindictively laid on her so savage a cramp that she almost fell.

For some time Dick hovered round the door of the attic, uncertain what he could do, and deeply disliking the place. At length he gathered his courage and squeezed under the door. Mrs Biddums had given Anne no rushlight, and she had not thought to ask; but it was a frosty moonlight night, and the moonshine streamed in at the window. There was a pallet bed on the floor, a plain wooden chest and three-legged stool. Anne had found the manchet and cream on the chest, and eaten it gratefully, taking the gift for Mrs Dimbleby's kindness. By the time Dick came in she had stored her few possessions in the chest, and was combing and brushing her pale gold hair – it had been almost white, he remembered, when she was a child. She kept herself resolutely from looking round, but she was alert for sounds, and started when the wainscot cracked. Dick drew back to the door when she knelt down, but when she had got into bed he came and knelt down beside her, resolved to watch with her until midnight had passed. At first she lay shivering in the cold bed and the clammy air of the attic. Then as she warmed a little she suddenly began to cry, burying her face in the pillow to stifle the sound. Hobberdy Dick, helpless and distracted, stroked her lightly, with fingers she did not know she could feel.

'Why did I come here!' she murmured as she cried. 'The Fettiplaces would be better than this. She can't be worse than this woman. I can't bear it! Don't be a fool, of course you can. The first day's the worst; it will be better tomorrow. Oh, I wish I was dead too, like everyone else!'

After a little while Dick's stroking brought back a faint cheerfulness. She turned over the pillow to find a dry side, and said in a shaky voice: 'Our Lord help me!' Then added, 'The old lady is very kind.'

Then, worn out with crying, she fell asleep. The air of horror in the room deepened as the time drew on to midnight, and the crying child appeared. Dick stayed bravely through the evil show, clinging to her bed. He did not want her to wake to it alone. But she slept through it all, overwearied by the day's troubles. At cockcrow the show faded and Dick went shakily from the room, too tired to inflict the promised pinching upon Mrs Widdison. That must wait till tomorrow. He went down to the kitchen fire, raked the embers together and fell asleep, twitching as he slept, and occasionally flicking an ear. Charity felt a shadowy something brush past her as she opened the door into the yard in the darkness of the December morning.

Anne was right; the first night was the most desolate of all. As she worked she found alleviations. Mrs Widdison was unreasonable and exacting and fitfully ostentatious, but she sometimes forgot that she was practising to be a great lady, and became more natural. If Anne could have flattered and gossiped she would soon have become a favourite, for the young woman was lonely. Mrs Biddums was steadily unkind, but Anne shared her unkindness with the rest of the household, and Mrs Dimbleby was as steadily kind. Anne had to teach the children music and fine embroidery, and though she was fond of children this was not an unmixed blessing. Rachel, who was the more apt at both lessons, imitated her mother, and was pert and rude; Martha, who liked her and whom she liked, hated fine work and had no fingers for the lute, though she sang tunefully enough. Little Samuel and the baby, who were her favourites, she only saw by chance, and she had no time in her busy life. But the chief alleviation of her lot was the goodwill of the house. She had always loved it; and, sad though it was to be inhabiting its empty shell, in the company of dear memories, it was kind to her still. And her work prospered. Mrs Widdison piled needlework on her, but if she left it, called away upon an errand, more was accomplished on her return than she remembered to have done. She would often come into Mrs Widdison's room to find it a dreary chaos of tumbled clothes and pomades and spilt cream; but as soon as she began to tidy it it righted itself to a marvel. Whatever she put her back to with a will seemed to swing into place. At first, when she found her sewing finished against all expectation she suspected that Mrs Dimbleby's kindness had been at work; but this could not often be possible. At length gradually there came on her the remembrance of the old stories of Hobberdy Dick; and still more dimly she remembered having seen him once as a tiny child when she had been in disgrace – a little dark man with prick ears, dressed in clothes as ragged as cobwebs. Then she knew that the good spirit of the house was there still, and her friend, and was glad that she had come back to the place.

Five

This ae night, this ae night,
  Every night and all.
Fire and sleet and candlelight,
And Christ receive thy saule.

The Lykewake Dirge

BUT if the days were happier for Anne, and for Hobberdy Dick too, the nights grew harder for both of them. It was getting near to Christmas, and until the twelve days of peace came, the forces of Winter grew stronger; ghosts and bogles pressed about the earth, and as the nights lengthened the lucifugi rose from their dark caverns and thronged about human ways. Dick found it increasingly hard to stand by his post in the attic; and evil dreams forced themselves even into Anne's over-wearied sleep. At last, one night, they woke her, and she sat up in bed with a beating heart, aware of a wicked thing in the room. There seemed a faint light at the end of the bed; more she could not see, but the room was icily cold, and cruelty and remorse and pain pressed on her like a weight, so that she could not move. She tried to say her prayers, but her tongue refused its utterance. Dick, who could see the whole show and fancied that she saw as much, was in pain for her as well as himself, but powerless. If this Christian human had no words of power from where could he gather them? He stepped forward, beating at the air with his thin arms, and the thing drew back a few paces under the weight of his courage, but there his power to help stopped. He had heard of men who died of the fear of what they saw; his Anne had courage he knew, but these human mortals were insecurely tethered to life; with a tug the rope would snap, and they would sail out of sight. He must fetch reinforcements; but where to go? He thought of the Taynton Lob and old Grim of Stow Churchyard, but after their defeat last May Day he had little confidence in them. Long George would never cross the Windrush on an errand to a stranger, and he was a witless fellow at best. What fools mortals were! They had not so much as a spayed bitch in a house with two ghosts in it. That at least would be some protection against spirits. What about human help? George Batchford was a sensible man and might know what to do, but nothing would induce him to set foot in the haunted attic at midnight. The old lady was the person. No evil spirit could stand against her.

He slipped aside from the pressure of the chill, foul air, and scrambled under the door. It was but a second before he was in Mrs Dimbleby's room, and by good fortune she was asleep. 'Come,' he said, too low to wake her, 'you're needed above-stairs.' He turned back the clothes, and helped her to rise. Her dark cloak was hanging on the door, and he gave it into her hand. She put it on, and put her feet into slippers and followed him steadily up the attic stairs, still in the light sleep of old age. She opened the door of the west attic, and Dick stood aside for her to go in, afraid of what he might see.

The Ur light was still in the room, but it lit nothing but itself. It was a moonless night, and Dick needed his night-piercing eyes to see Anne, risen a little from the bed, pressed against the wall with her hand to her throat. Mrs Dimbleby's eyes were shut, but apparently she saw the ghost as well as Dick did himself. She stood

53

for a moment turned towards it, and then said in a voice even lower than usual, 'You poor, wicked thing, come out of the shadow of the poor child, and let it join his soul. What good does it do you to chew over and over again the evil things you did? You'll be none the better of it. Come out, and go to the place that is best for you, through the love of God.'

Gently as the words were spoken they went through Hobberdy Dick like fire, driving him backward and almost consuming his being. He had no power for a moment to look at the creature to whom they were addressed; but cowered outside the open door of the attic, beaten almost to the ground. In a moment, however, strength, and even merriment, flared up in him again. He gave a loud ho! ho! and sprang up to the top of the door, where he swung to and fro. The noise he made, and Anne's gasp of relief, wakened the old lady, but she waked to healthy darkness and the wholesome chill of the winter's night.

'Where am I?' she said, swaying a little in the darkness. Dick sprang down to her support, and Anne jumped from the bed to take her arm and guide her to the stool.

'Don't be frightened,' she said. 'You're in my attic.'

'I must have walked up in my sleep,' said Mrs Dimbleby. 'I thought I was needed somewhere. I am afraid I frightened you.'

'No, no, I was so glad to have you come in. It is cold here. Shall I take you down to your room, or will you lie in my bed here?'

'I had better go downstairs or you will have nowhere to sleep; but I should be glad if you would help me.'

Anne helped her carefully downstairs, shivering and very weak. She put her to bed, then ran down to the kitchen, where Dick had already blown up the fire, and heated a brick in the embers to wrap in flannels and put to her feet. Then she warmed some milk for her in a skillet, and sat by her rubbing her until the shivering had passed.

'My dear, you must go to bed. Young people need their sleep, and you have a full day in front of you,' said Mrs Dimbleby.

'May I sit by you a little while?' said Anne. 'I should like to be here.'

She sat by her till the turn of the night, and dozed there until it was time to go up to her attic to dress. The maids were struggling into their clothes as she went through the dormitory. She shut the door behind her, put her rushlight on the chest, and looked round the little room with a thankful heart.

'This place will be a refuge to me from now on,' she thought. 'I shall never be afraid to be here again.'

Six

And leading us, makes us to stray
Long winter nights out of the way,
And when we stick in mire and clay,
He doth with laughter leave us.

DRAYTON, *Nymphidia*

ANNE wakened on the next morning after that to a
world of clear shining frost. It was two days before the
Eve of one of the most dismal Christmases England had
known. Only the geese had reason to rejoice. Above-
stairs Mr Widdison had decreed a strict Puritan
Christmas, without so much as a mince pie; below-
stairs old Ursula's presence enjoined a perpetual fast;
but George Batchford did not mean to be completely cheated of his Christmas. When Anne ran out
to fetch clean spring water for Mrs Widdison's morning
draught she saw him looming dimly through the frost,
like old Christmas himself, with a great bundle of
holly on his shoulders.

'Is the house to be trimmed after all?' she asked him
in some surprise.

'Nay, Mistress Seckar,' said George Batchford. 'The
Master be too set in new-fangled ways for that; but
that's not to say the stables and cowsheds shan't have
their share of what's right; so I've took time by the
fetlock, as ye might say, and gathered my hollins early,
so as I can deck the place at odd moments. Yes, and
there'll be a yule log burning in the old oast-house on
Christmas Eve, so ruinated as it be, and crabs to roast
and nuts to crack for those as can be there.'

56

'Can you give me a sprig or two of holly, and a red apple,' said Anne, 'and a piece of the mistletoe that grows in the old Worcester Pearmain just by the beehives, and I'll make you a kissing ring to hang in the stable. I know just the place where it should hang.'

'That's a good little lady,' said George Batchford heartily. '"Twill bring luck to the cattle; for the good-will of the place is with you, if 'twas ever with any. I'll get them right away, and give them to Charity for you when she comes out to gather the eggs.'

'And will you set aside a pottle of milk for me to make a treacle posset for Mrs Dimbleby? She has a heavy chill, and nothing seems to warm her.'

'That I will, Mistress Seckar,' said George Batchford, who had fallen into the way of treating Anne as the lady of the house; and Anne hurried back with her tall crystal flagon to call Mrs Widdison. She found time when she went down for Mrs Widdison's fresh-aired smock to heat a treacle posset and run up with it to Mrs Dimbleby's room. Mrs Dimbleby was moving slowly about dressing, without any trace of the old light alacrity.

'Won't you stay in bed a little longer, Madam?' said Anne. 'Here is a hot posset for you, and I will bring you something to eat later.'

'Thank you, my dear, but I will come down to prayers. There's naught amiss with me but a kind of numbness, and that's the better for movement.'

But to Hobberdy Dick, who had followed Anne into the room, leaving George Batchford and his holly, it seemed that her rope was wearing thin, and might snap at any moment. He sat behind the curtains of her bed and watched her anxiously as she sipped her posset. In a moment, however, he heard Mrs Biddums' voice raised in the best bedroom, and slipped out, as alert as a weasel, to see what was the matter.

'I've missed this and that,' old Ursula was saying, 'but when it comes to dipping into my treacle jar, and simmering milk on the hob as bold as brass, then 'tis time to speak. 'Twill be sack and sugar next.'

'I think, madam,' said Anne, 'you should call Mr Silvester, the apothecary, to see Mrs Dimbleby. She was walking in her sleep two nights ago, and it seems to have struck a chill on her that nothing will warm. I looked in on her this morning, and took her up a treacle posset; but I am afraid she is beyond kitchen physic.'

'If she wants anything why can't she send down to Mrs Biddums for it?' said Mrs Widdison. 'You're my gentlewoman, and I'll thank you to attend to me, and not go rambling about the house as if you owned it, seeing to this and that.'

Mr Widdison came in at the clamour of voices.

'What's all this to-do?' he said. 'I can get no quiet to look over the passage of Scripture I'm to read. What's amiss?'

'This pert girl takes it on her to say your Mother-in-law is ill, and to go treating her to treacle posset and what not on her own motion.'

'It struck me yesterday,' said Mr Widdison, 'that she looked mortal pale and still. I wouldn't have her miscarry for all the place is worth. I'll send one of the men to Burford for the potecary.'

'Depend upon it, it's no more than a chill,' said Mrs Widdison. 'And if she'd said a word to Ursula here she'd have had all the care she needed. She's never ailing.'

'She's not one to complain,' said Mr Widdison, 'but she's never been so to call lusty. And she's been as good as a mother to me ever since she came to nurse my pretty Nan through her last illness. I'll send one of the men after breakfast.'

Hobberdy Dick could see that Mrs Widdison was ill pleased by this reference to the first wife, and old Ursula, who belonged to Mrs Widdison's side of the house, tossed her head and muttered; but Mr Widdison was the Master. Old Mrs Dimbleby was sent back to bed, and one of the men rode across to Burford to fetch Mr Silvester, who had some reputation as an apothecary. He could find little wrong with the old lady; but the spring of life seemed broken, and she was all at once very weak. She lay quiet and smiling in her bed. The maids, when they could evade Mrs Biddums, slipped in with tit-bits and offers of service. Martha sat and read to her in a monotonous sing-song. Hobberdy Dick neglected George Batchford's Christmas preparations in the oast-house, and hung uneasily about her door. He would have come nearer, but the cloud in which she lay had grown perilously bright. Fascinated and terrified he hovered on the outskirts, and peered at her through it. There was little he could do for her; but the maids found pipkins of cream and pieces of manchet ready to carry up to her in places where old Ursula had never set them. They availed themselves of the opportunity without inquiry. Only the greediest of them, Maria Parminter, ate one of them herself, and she suffered dreadfully that night from cramps and nightmare.

The illness was so gentle that till Christmas had come and gone no one but Hobberdy Dick and Mrs Dimbleby herself knew the event, though Anne was uneasy. She would gladly have spent more time with Mrs Dimbleby, who loved to hear her sing and play; but Mrs Widdison found the cold weather and muddy lanes depressing, and needed continual attention.

So Tuesday went and Wednesday, and Thursday was Christmas Eve. Christmas Day was ordained as a fast day among the stricter of the sects, and Samuel Widdison, who wished to gain a good name among his Puritan neighbours, was determined to treat it so. There was to be no service, for that would be a Papistical observance, but a weekday lecture and prayer meeting was to be held in the great room of the Bear Inn at Burford, and in a barn at Swinbrook. Samuel decided to attend the Burford meeting himself, and send his family to Swinbrook. On Christmas Eve Mr Dods, one of the local preachers, came to dine; and when he had departed after long prayers Mr Widdison tried to get his wife early to bed, an attempt in which he was heartily seconded by all the household. By half past ten the whole household seemed to be lapped in slumber, by eleven the greater part of it was stirring again. Old Ursula was snoring in her attic; and the three maids, with their shoes in their hands, went tiptoeing down the creaky stairs. The baby was bundled up warmly by the nursemaid and carried down, lest he should wake and cry. Rachel and Diligence, the oldest and youngest of the girls, went down with the nursemaid; Martha waited till the sound of talking had stopped in the best room, and deep breathing had succeeded it; then stole in to fetch Samuel away, who was lying wide-eyed and staring in his truckle bed. It was against the counsel of the rest that she did it, for they were afraid the Widdisons would be awakened; but with the help of Hobberdy Dick it was successfully accomplished. Soon hooded figures were stealing across the yard towards the distant oast-house, from whose open door came the flicker of firelight. Dick turned

aside to the stables to swing in his kissing ring, which
Anne had hung just in his favourite spot. He was
touched to find that someone still remembered his old
ways; but between Mrs Dimbleby and the preparations
for Christmas he had had little time to play with his
present. Now he swung there with a thankful heart,
remembering the meagre Christmas of a year ago, when
old Peacock had crouched sadly over the rotten piece
of wood that had served him for a yule log. He had
not swung long before the stars turned towards twelve
o'clock. In a few minutes the cattle would be upon
their knees. Already a cool, sweet air of Paradise was
blowing through the stable. Beyond the earthly wind
that was chasing the clouds across the moon he heard
superlunary music, as the moving spheres rang their
Christmas chime. He jumped from his ring and ran out
into the yard. This interplanetal accordance was not for
him, and he made his way to the easier and more pagan
merriment of the oast-house. The scene there was one
to warm his heart. The old oast-house was partly in
ruins, but it had a sound earth floor, beaten hard by
generations of wear. George Batchford had filled in
the gaps in the wall with hurdles covered with sacks
and hidden by armfuls of holly. Holly was stuck into
the chinks in the masonry, and a great bunch of mistletoe swung high from a long stick wedged into the wall.
Fir torches, hammered into the floor, flickered in the
wind. The room was draughty enough, but a huge
fire roared on the hearth, and all inside were too busy
and merry to feel the cold.

There must have been more than a score of people
in the room, for convivial labourers had come from
the farms round, where a stricter supervision had been
kept. Martha, Diligence, little Samuel, Ned the house-
boy, Charity and half a dozen others were playing at

hot cockles. Rachel, Maria Parminter and Nancy, the oldest of the maids, were roasting chestnuts and crab-apples, the butler, Jonathon Fletcher, a grave, silent man, was brewing a bowl of lambswool in which the crabs were to float, a group of lads at the far end of the room were improvising clothes for the mumming play, George Batchford, with a cushion on his head to mark his rank as King of the Revels, was directing everyone, his usually gloomy and impassive face aglow with good humour, and the nips he had taken to quicken his spirits. Hobberdy Dick unperceived added his own ho! ho! ho! to the sound of merriment which went up from the place, and slipped into a dark corner beyond the fire, from which he could watch all that went on. Presently the mummers, with blackened faces and gay tags fluttering about them, came stamping in from the far end of the room, and one of them, with a broom in his hand, swept the dust in behind the door for luck.

> Here come I, sent on before,
> To sweep the dust behind the door,

he chanted. Then Father Christmas came on, and the King from Wessex, and the dragon, with a flail wag-ging behind him for a tail, the Bessie, with a cloak pinned round him for a skirt, and an apron borrowed from one of the girls, and the Fool, with straw in his hair. It was a hotch-potch of a play, for several tradi-tions met there, and everyone made up his part as it suited him; but it was received with great applause, and the girls laughed till their sides ached. Then some of the lads, who had been peering over the heads of the others, dragged a big log into the centre of the circle, and began to play at pulling Dun from the Mire, lift-ing and straining with loud 'gerrups', and trying each man to drop the log on the toes of his fellows, until, when they were all straining their hardest, George Batchford, as Beelzebub, gave it a sudden push forward, and the whole line fell down, among louder laughter than ever.

Some of the older men were playing Post and Pair with an old and very tattered pack of cards, but the rest were gathered round in a circle to watch the more active games, for Shoe the Wild Mare had now succeeded Dun in the Mire. Presently the unlatched door was pushed open, and Anne came quietly into the room.

'You're welcome, mistress,' said George Batchford, rising from his state. 'Are you come to play a turn with us?'

'I can't leave Mrs Dimbleby long untended,' said Anne. 'But I came to wish a happy Christmas to us all.'

'The lambswool is ready, we only waited for you,' said George Batchford. 'Bring it forward, Mr Fletcher. But if you will wait a minute before we pledge it round I have someone here who will put a gilt to it.'

He left the oast-house, and in a minute the listeners heard the beat of a tabor and a song coming nearer:

> Wassail, wassail all over the town,
> Our bread it is white and our ale it is brown;
> Wassail to the great and wassail to the less,
> And joy be to all on this fair Christmesse.

George Batchford proudly led old Hugh Powell into the room, the half-blind singer, who boasted that his father had been a bard from Wales and had played to Queen Elizabeth on her first progress. His mother had been a gipsy from Wychwood, cast off by her people on her marriage, and their child had wandered over the length of the country until persecution and the hard times had driven him to take refuge in a ruined lodge

in Wychwood, where few knew where to find him. His
dog had been shot by the troopers, and he himself had
only escaped by flight from being swum as a wizard.
Now he went out seldom and by night, accompanied
only by a friendly Will o' the Wisp, who could do little
to guide his blinded way, but was attracted by his
music. Dick saw it now through the open door, hover-
ing palely beyond the light cast by the fire and torches.

Old Powell was welcomed by the whole room, and
given a few sips of the wassail bowl as he sat in the
warmest corner by the fire, and drummed on his tabor
and sang random snatches of the wassail song:

> Now here's to the butler with his red nose,
> May he brew us good liquor wherever he goes;
> Sherry sack for the great and good ale for the less,
> And joy be to all on this fair Christmesse.

The roasted crabs were plunged in the bowl, George
Batchford took a ceremonial sip and handed it to
Anne. She drank to the company, and handed it back
to George Batchford with a curtsey to the King of the
Revels. Then, with a 'Merry Christmas to all here', she
left the room. All felt that the gentry had visited them
and left them to their revels. The bowl went round
merrily to the accompaniment of the tabor. When it
was empty Hugh Powell struck up an invitation to the
dance:

> One, two, come buckle your shoe,
> Three, four, there's guests at the door,

mounting by pairs until at 'Nineteen, twenty, now
we've plenty' he burst into The Beginning of the
World, and all danced according to their capacity.
Hobberdy Dick joined in with a snapping of fingers
and an undercurrent of mouth music, until he was

suddenly checked by Willy Wisp, who had ventured as near as he could to the door, and was pointing with a blue and tremulous finger into the darkness. Hob darted out to join him. A distant lantern was wavering across the yard from the open door of the Manor, and behind it Hobberdy Dick recognized Mr Widdison. There was not a moment to be lost, or their Christmas revels would be broken up into a most painful disorder. Dick snatched the blue light from the tips of Willy Wisp's fingers, who at once snapped them smartly together and re-lit it. At the same time he mustered his half-forgotten power, and, stooping a little, he scooped a palmful of muddy water from the nearest puddle with his left hand, and threw it scatteringly behind his back, with a mutter of 'pitter-patter, holy-water'. A thick mist rose behind him, blotting out the light that streamed from the oast-house. Against it his own light stood out sharply and undimmed. Willy Wisp, with his blue fingers flickering, pattered loyally to his side.

Samuel Widdison had waked at about half-past twelve to a sense of unwonted peace. It was not so much that the house was comparatively free from human company, but that he was resting on a bed freed for a time from the thoughts of money. It was the first night of Christmas, and the ghost had taken his money bags with him and gone to some obscure refrigidarium of his own. For the first time for nearly twelve months Samuel awakened without a thought of gain. He had been dreaming of his young first wife, Nan Dimbleby, with her pretty, quiet ways, and of the great beaupots of flowers with which she had scented their close city rooms. He fancied at first that she was sleeping beside him, and turned towards his second wife. The scent from her pomades seemed for a moment to come from one of Nan's bouquets. Then he remembered who she was, and lay thinking of her with a kind of dispassionate protectiveness, for she was a good wife to him in her way, and a kind mother to the children. 'To all except my Joel,' he thought, and his mind dwelt fondly on the boy, and on the way in which he had settled into the country as if he was born to be a squire. He would like the lad at home, he thought, but he was safer in London for the present. It would never do to take up with the wrong set at first. Then the air of Christmas blew on him again, and he thought of Joel and his Nan and old Mrs Dimbleby together, three dear to him and yet strange, native to a world in which he was a stranger, or not so much a stranger as an alienated and disinherited child of the soil. These thoughts never remained with him until day; thoughts of gain and thriving and good repute thronged his mind then, and by night the haunted bed held him to the same strain. But at odd times when the spell was lifted he knew for a short blink what his soul desired. He lay for a little, rested and happy, and then distaste for himself and his usual way of life made him restless, and desire for action drove him to get up and see if Mrs Dimbleby wanted anything. He took down his greatcoat from the door, thrust his feet into his slippers, and went silently out of the room.

The door of Mrs Dimbleby's closet was open, and the flickering light of a candle came from it. Anne Seckar was in the room, giving the old lady something hot to drink. The quiet candlelight, the curve of Anne's figure as she bent over the bed, and the low murmur of affectionate talk made the scene intimate and withdrawn, so that Mr Widdison felt more than ever an alien, and turned away. He paced to the end of the passage, and drew back the curtains to look at the night. He thought he would wait a few moments, and ask Anne when she came out how the old lady was; but when he looked out the idea was driven from his mind. It was a moonlight night, with a small moon, fitfully covered by clouds, but it was not only the moon that illuminated the yard. From somewhere beyond the stables there was a red glow. The cares of the daytime world crowded back again into Mr Widdison's mind. He thought of robbers and of fire, and hurried downstairs to waken Jonathon and the boy. Their pallets were pulled out of the cupboard, but empty. Samuel Widdison hardly knew how to believe it, but it almost seemed as if some, in his quiet and Puritan household, had stolen out to Christmas revelry. His anger mounted. He found a candle lantern and lit it, and took up a stout stick. Then in a lucky moment for himself he noticed his best suit, well brushed for the morrow, hanging on a chair by the fire to air. He pulled on the galligaskins over his nightshirt, saw his uncleaned boots in the scullery and drew them on, then opened the kitchen door, and started across the windy yard. Almost at once the scene changed. From above, the yard had been plain to see except when the clouds covered the moon; but after a few steps his way was obscured by a white, woolly mist. In front of him he could see a faint light still, and he made angrily towards it; but it was further away than he had supposed, and he must somehow have wavered in his course, for it seemed to have moved to his right hand. He turned towards it, and now he had plunged deep into the mist, so that he could see nothing but the light faintly in front. What was strange was that he trod upon twigs that crackled sharply. He looked behind him, and saw a faint blue light which could only shine from his kitchen door. He knew that as long as he kept in the straight path between these two lights he could not go astray, so he plunged forward boldly, angered by a faint sound of laughter in front of him. It seemed that he went an immense distance, but he put it down to the effect of the blanketing mist, until he suddenly stepped into the little stream that ran down into the Windrush. There was a loud ho! ho! quite near to him, and for the first time it struck him that he was following a lantern held by some escaping thief. Samuel Widdison was no coward; but the blanket of mist, his ignorance of his whereabouts and the uncanny laughter in front of him, put him into a panic, and he turned round towards the fainter light, to make his way back to the house. It seemed he had gone further than he thought, for he walked an immense way, and the light grew no nearer. When he looked over his shoulder the first light still shone steadily behind him. What confounded him most was the inequality of the ground, far greater than the frozen ruts of his own yard. If he could but come upon a wall it would give him something to follow; but though he felt that he had been walking for miles he could come across none. He hesitated, grasped his stick more firmly and turned back towards the brighter light. Almost at once he stumbled over a fallen branch that he had not passed before, broke some surface ice and floundered into a patch of boggy ground. When he had pulled himself out again he had left one boot behind.

Seven

Whilst in this mill wee labour and turne round
As in a conjurers circle, William found
A menes for our deliverence; Turne your cloakes,
Quoth hee, for Puck is busy with these oakes.

CORBET, *Iter Borealis*

IN the meantime the Christmas festivities had come
merrily to their appointed end and with cautious fare-
wells the party had separated. George Batchford took
Hugh Powell up to the stable loft, to sleep with him
for what remained of the night, Jonathon and the
boy tumbled into their pallet beds, the maids stole
tittering up the attic stairs, Samuel got into bed with
his sisters, the guests took their various ways in small
parties, noting and avoiding the thick patch of mist
which hung over the water meadows and coppice upstream. The whole dispersal was managed successfully;
but the baby who had been happily asleep for the past
hour, woke and cried as he was laid in the cold sheets.
Mrs Widdison's sleep had been already disturbed by
the small noises of re-occupation in the house, and at
last the sound waked her. She stretched out her hand
to touch her husband, and found the bed beside her
empty and cold. She lay for a while expecting his return, and when nothing happened became increasingly alarmed. At length she put a cloak about her,
took up the unlit candle, and went down to the kitchen
to blow up the fire, and light it.

Jonathon Fletcher had hardly fallen asleep before

he was shaken awake again, and found Mrs Widdison standing agitated by his side.

'The master isn't in the house,' she cried. 'I've searched everywhere, and he's not here. He must be murdered. Find him. Find him quickly.'

Jonathon Fletcher woke slowly, a little confused with the lambswool he had taken, for he was a temperate man as a rule. When at last he understood what she said he was still disinclined for action.

'Don't you fret yourself, mistress,' he said. 'Maybe the master wouldn't thank us for looking for him. Belike he's gone off to the Christmas revels somewhere.'

'How dare you say such a thing, Jonathon Fletcher,' said his mistress, stamping in her agitation. 'Get on your things this minute, and go and rouse that great surly clodpole, George Batchford, to look too. Make them drag the river. I'll not rest a minute till he's found.'

By this time the whole house was astir, even old Ursula, who despaired at once, and put the whole thing down to this silly notion of living in the country. Jonathon dressed while the boy ran to call George Batchford, and tell him what had happened. George Batchford, who had been talking to Hugh Powell in the stable loft, came down at his call, and climbed the ladder in some bewilderment to ask old Powell's advice.

'Here's a pretty caddle,' he said. 'It seems the master've been lifted out of his bed, drawed clean away from madam's side and she never the wiser. What do you make of that, Master Hugh? It don't seem natural like on the first night of Christmas.'

'It don't,' said Powell. 'What sort of man is this Widdison?'

'Oh, he've no great sense, and he's not a hearty man,

but I should ha' said there was no great harm in he. I wouldn't have thought the fiend would have had any power over him on a night like this.'

'Set my foot on the ladder,' said Hugh Powell. 'And maybe I can see the way it is. Didn't someone say there was a mist over the water meadows? And it a windy night and frosty.'

George Batchford led him carefully to the top of the ladder, and went down it ahead of him. Once on the ground, old Powell found his way out of the stable without difficulty.

'Now look out, George, and tell if there be a mist on the water meadow as they said.'

'Aye, a pocket of thick mist not much bigger nor the oast-house.'

'Look again, and see if you can make out a light in the midst of it.'

'It seems to me,' said George after a pause, 'like there's two lights, the one a smartish way off from t'other.'

'Then depend upon it, George, he's Pouk-ledden, and you can get him clear if you will.'

'I don't know about that,' said George Batchford. 'He've crossed the luck of the place one way and another, and maybe 'twill be none too easy to win him clear, nor lucky neither to attempt it. Still, he's the master, though 'tis little he knows, and I suppose I must fetch him home if I can.'

'Maybe it won't be necessary for you to go into the mist at all; but take a crust of bread in your pocket in case. If you halloo from the edge may be he'll hear you, and you can bid him turn his coat. And good luck go with you for a faithful servant.'

Jonathon Fletcher was hardly dressed, and stood confused by his mistress's laments and old Ursula's shrill objurgations, when George Batchford came into the kitchen, broke the kissing crust off a loaf set on the dresser by the maids in their hasty preparation of restoratives, put it into his pocket, and went out again into the darkness. Presently his voice could be heard raised at a little distance. 'Hallo there, Master! Is that you?'

Hobberdy Dick was glad to hear George Batchford's voice, for he was getting tired of his sport, and only kept it up till he was sure that all trace of the Christmas revels had been obliterated. He blew the mist aside as George came up, and Samuel Widdison saw the ray from the human lantern, a warmer glow than the blue light he had been following for so long. However he was too worn out by this time to make towards it. Besides, his bare foot was cut and sore, and he was forespent. He called a faint answer to George Batchford's shout.

'Be that you, master?' said George Batchford. 'Turn your coat, man, and ye'll win clear easy enough.'

'I shall do nothing so superstitious or ridiculous,' said Samuel Widdison, faintly but with spirit. 'If the powers of evil are unloosed here tonight, as I have reason to believe they may be, I'll not truckle to them with superstitious usages.'

'Don't you be too sure they're the powers of evil,' said George Batchford. 'Such don't have no sway on a night like this. But if 'twas the powers of good, maybe you and me would fare as ill. Turn your coat, master, and make for my lantern.'

But Samuel Widdison, shaken though he was, was still too much himself to give way on such a point. Between cold and fatigue he was only half conscious, and at length George Batchford made his way through the rapidly thinning mist, took off his own coat, and wrapped it, inside out, round Mr Widdison's shoulders. Dick, always pleased to see the old usages observed, gave a loud laugh and made off towards the kitchen. He too had had a cold and exhausting night. The kitchen was too crowded for comfort, and he slipped out again, to rake up the ashes in the oast-house, and have a much needed nap. As he went out Samuel Widdison came limping into the house on George Batchford's arm. He was met by Mrs Widdison, whose anxiety was rapidly passing into anger.

'What do you mean by leaving your bed and slipping away, to come back in such a state?'

'I shall have to ask that question of others,' said Samuel Widdison. 'But give me something hot quickly, for I am chilled to death.'

He shivered as he spoke, and looked so wretched that Mrs Widdison suspended her anger for the time, and hurried him up to bed, followed by old Ursula with a hot posset. Anne had put hot bricks into the bed, and after sneezing and shivering for a little he fell asleep. The whole household was glad to do the same, though it was by this time morning. George Batchford fed the stock and milked the cow, and tumbled up to the loft again, determined to make Christmas a day of rest, if he could do no more. In a couple of hours, however, the household was astir again, for old Ursula would not let them rest. Even Hobberdy Dick was disturbed, for George Batchford came into the oast-house to remove all traces of the night's revels. Jonathon Fletcher followed him there, looking pale and anxious, with a racking headache.

'A pretty pickle you've landed us in, George Batchford,' he said, 'with your Christmas sports and heathen mummeries. I don't know how I came to be so led away as to consent to it. From what the master said before he went up to bed he'd been down and found our beds empty, and gone out to seek us. Dear knows why he didn't find us then and there, but he'll rout out the story, and then we shall all be sent packing.'

'He'll never turn you off with the story you have to tell to he,' said George Batchford.

'What story? We haven't a leg to stand on.'

'Why, tell 'un as you wakened and heard a noise, and saw a light, and took out the boy to see what it might be, and then you wandered up and down and didn't seem able to find your way back, till you wakened in your own bed, and thought 'twas no more than a dream.'

'You can't tell that kind of tale to the master. He's city bred, same as I am, and would no more believe me than if I was to tell him I'd been out riding a unicorn.'

'That's the story he'll believe today, and no other,' said George Batchford. 'Try 'un and see.'

Hobberdy Dick was amused by this talk, and curious to hear what Jonathon's explanation would be. He followed him into the house, and found the whole place at odds. There was hardly a soul in it that was not as cross as two sticks. Mrs Dimbleby's room was the only place where tranquillity still dwelt. There was no Christmas church-going to set people to rights, and all over the house there were headaches and heavy eyes. Old Ursula scolded as if she were an eight-day nagging machine newly wound up, little Samuel was whining and Martha forgot her usual good humour so far as to slap him. In his bedroom Mr Widdison was sneezing and blowing his nose, with his feet in a strong bath of mustard. Mrs Widdison was standing by, scolding.

'It's the meanness and deceit I mind most,' she was saying as Dick slipped into the room. 'To huddle me away to bed under pretence of being too strict for any

74

gaieties, and then to go off on a drinking bout, and to come back so drunk that you couldn't find your way across your own fields! And think of the disgrace of it among the neighbours! It's sure to come out through the servants. A pretty picture you were when you came in!'

'I tell you it was nothing of the sort,' said Samuel Widdison. 'I suppose you'd like me to creep under the bedclothes and let the house be robbed. I tell you I saw a light and heard noises, and the servants weren't in their beds; so I went out to see what was the matter, and got lost in the mist.'

'If I told a lie, which Heaven forbid!' said his wife, 'I should take care to invent a better one than that.'

'So should I,' said Samuel Widdison. 'Now I've heard enough from you. Go and tell Jonathon Fletcher I want to speak with him. I'll hear what he has to say for himself.'

Mrs Widdison tossed her head as she left the room; but her anger was by now more than half pretended, for her anxiety was completely allayed, and she knew that she had a powerful weapon against her husband. She had never held him at such an advantage before. Hobberdy Dick, sitting on the tester of the bed, looked down on Mr Widdison with some compunction, but he thought his education was beginning at last. Jonathon Fletcher appeared in the doorway, evidently ill at ease, and waited for what his master had to say. Mr Widdison sneezed several times; then he said tartly: 'What excuse can you give for being out of your bed last night when I called you?'

'Well, Master,' said Jonathon, looking round the room for inspiration. 'It was a thing the like of which never happened to me before. I seemed to see a light and hear the sound of talking and laughing beyond the

75

stables, and I went out across the yard, and then I hardly knew how the time went. I seemed to be dancing about, as you might say, and going to and fro, and there was noises and lights all round me. And then presently the mistress shook me. But as for you calling me, Master, I never heard a thing.'

'How can you expect me –' began Samuel Widdison angrily, and then broke off. ''Tis strange,' he muttered. 'That's enough, Jonathon. Don't let it happen again.'

Outside the door Jonathon wiped the damp palms of his hands on his apron. He had a superstition against telling a downright lie, and felt with relief that he had not said a word that was not true. Samuel Widdison sneezed, and stared thoughtfully at the steaming yellow water. Something had happened which he did not understand.

Eight

O where will I get a bonny boy,
Will win gold to his fee,
And will run unto Childe Yvet
With this letter from me?

Old Ballad

THE days of Christmas went quietly on. Samuel Widdison's cold kept him to the house, and he saw to it that there was no Christmas merry-making. The maids honoured the season by doing as little work as they could; but even here their desire outran their performance. Anne was kept busy, however, covering their omissions, and at night Hobberdy Dick worked hard to finish the tasks they had abandoned. Thanks to these two, things went moderately well, though old Mrs Dimbleby's soothing presence was missed increasingly.

By Twelfth Night Mr Widdison's cold was better, and he had leisure to observe that Mrs Dimbleby was far weaker than she had been at the beginning of Christmastide. She lay, hardly moving, in her bed, and could not speak above a whisper. He grew suddenly alarmed about her.

'Come, Mother,' he said, with unaccustomed tenderness. 'You must perk up a little for all our sakes. The house doesn't seem like itself without you. Is there anything I can get you that you would like?'

'You are very kind, my dear,' she murmured. 'If it did not put you about too much I should dearly like to see Joel.'

'That you shall, Mother. I'll send up to town and find out how business is, and if we're not too pressed he shall come down.'

'It will need to be soon if I am to see him; for I don't think I shall have to stay here for more than a few days longer.'

'Have to stay! But haven't we made you happy here?'

'You have been a kind son to me always, Samuel, but there are things my heart pants to see. Ever since I heard the pass-word spoken, and knew that I might go it seems I can hardly stay my feet.'

They were interrupted by the entrance of Mrs Widdison.

'Here's company for you, Mrs Dimbleby! My Lady Fettiplace has rid over to ask if she may see you. Shall we put on your lace cap and black silk gown, and you can sit in the chair by the fire?'

'No, no,' said Mr Widdison. 'She is not fit to see anyone but ourselves. Tell my lady so, with our thanks.'

'I should like to see her,' said Mrs Dimbleby, 'but I know she'll excuse my rising. Thanks to your care, my dear, the room is always neat and fresh. Show her up, and I'll have a tell with her, poor young thing.'

Mrs Widdison hesitated and looked doubtful, but her husband said: 'Do as she says, my dear. She best knows what she is fit for.'

He followed her out of the room to say, – 'I fear she is sicker than we thought for, and I'll go down and write a note to Joel to come, and have it ready to send if the potecary thinks as ill of her as I do.'

'It's not come to that yet,' said Mrs Widdison. 'Old folks will have their fancies.' But she bit off her speech short, and went into the Withdrawing Room to beg Lady Fettiplace to walk upstairs.

Mr Widdison turned aside into his office, the Rent Room, as Mrs Widdison proudly called it, a small, dark room where he went over his accounts, and wrote his London letters. Hobberdy Dick followed him eagerly, and watched him mend his pen and write a short note to Joel.

He pondered for a little; then he called for a candle, sealed and indited it, and locked it in the travelling desk where he kept his papers. Dick would have been better pleased to see it dispatched out of hand, but if it was not to go immediately it was perhaps safer locked away from Mrs Widdison's interference. That done, he called the boy for a light for his pipe, and when he had brought it sent him running to Burford to ask Mr Silvester to look in on them if he had business that way, and sup with them that night if it pleased him.

When he sat down to smoke Dick recollected his curiosity about the conversation between Mrs Dimbleby and Lady Fettiplace; but he had a certain awe about intruding on them which made him linger outside the door, and watch Mrs Widdison fluttering from the Withdrawing Room to the stairs, curious like him, and like him unable to make her way into the room. When the bedroom door opened Mrs Widdison scurried hastily into the Withdrawing Room, and in a moment Anne went upstairs to escort Lady Fettiplace down.

'My mistress would be honoured,' she said with a curtsey, 'if you would drink a glass of wine by the fire before you go out again into the cold.'

'I think you must be the young gentlewoman of whom Mrs Dimbleby told me,' said Lady Fettiplace, quickly and low. 'I should like to hold some talk with you at some time if I may.'

'Very willingly,' said Anne, 'but will you come to

Mrs Widdison now?' She led Lady Fettiplace to the Withdrawing Room door; then, since the house boy had gone on Mr Widdison's errand, she brought in wine and small cakes, and asked Jonathon to let Mr Widdison know that Lady Fettiplace was taking wine with them. However, by the time Samuel Widdison had knocked out his pipe Lady Fettiplace had sipped her wine, and was in the hall, ready to mount. Mr Widdison led her to the door.

'Your mother-in-law is happy to know that her grandson is coming to see her,' she said as they went. 'If you have any difficulty in sending to London I send daily to my lord, who is up there at present, and should have much pleasure in instructing my servant to see your note delivered.'

'I thank you, my lady,' said Mr Widdison. 'But I will see first what the physician says. My son is much engaged, and I should be loth for him to break off his employment before there is need.'

He bowed, and turned in to the house. Hobberdy Dick lingered outside, sniffing the air. It seemed to him that he smelt snow on its way, and if Joel did not come in a day or two the roads might well be blocked. He hoped that Mr Silvester would be prompt in his coming and quick-sighted when he came. He was kept in suspense the rest of the day, for darkness fell before there was any news of Mr Silvester, and it was not till five o'clock that a note came from him. Mr Widdison read it, and went into the parlour, where Mrs Widdison was sitting at embroidery among the girls, and Dick in a dark corner was putting the silks of Anne's tapestry to rights, which had been tumbled and tangled by little Sam.

'How do you think my mother-in-law seems this evening?' he said. 'I have a note from Mr Silvester to say he has but just returned from a funeral at Stow, and will do himself the honour of calling on us to-morrow if our case be not urgent. His messenger stays for our answer.'

'Oh there is no urgency,' said Mrs Widdison. 'I have but just come down from seeing her, and she seems quite at ease, and disposed to sleep. If she had been really ill she would not have been so ready to see my Lady Fettiplace this morning.'

'I don't know, I don't know,' said Mr Widdison. 'I'm uneasy about her. But I'd be loth to discommode Mr Silvester after his cold journey.'

'Tomorrow will be time enough,' said Mrs Widdison decidedly.

Mr Widdison turned back into the hall to give a verbal message to Mr Silvester's servant. Dick glowered from his dark corner at Mrs Widdison and slipped out to snuff the weather again. The snow would be on them, he thought, in two or three days, and there was Mr Widdison's letter lying doing nothing in his desk. It struck Dick that it was time he took a hand, but he must wait till the household was abed, for Mr Widdison's pocket was not easily picked. They seemed to him an unconscionable time in getting to bed that night, but in the end the last candle was blown out, and only the kitchen embers glowed in the dark house, for it was a moonless night, still and cold. Dick crept into the best bedroom, slipped his hand under Mr Widdison's pillow and drew out the keys. The ghost looked up sharply, here was a loss with which he could sym-pathise, but Dick nodded reassurance, and slid down the bannisters to Mr Widdison's rent room. The desk was standing as usual on the heavy long table in the corner; and it took Dick less than a minute to unlock it, take out the letter, lock the desk again and run upstairs. Before the ghost had counted out twenty Harry sovereigns he was back again with the keys and had replaced them under the pillow; not long after he was in the stable.

Out of respect for Hobberdy Dick, George Batchford kept no bored flints hanging over the stalls, so Dick had no difficulty in scrambling on to the back of the best horse, a stout and steady cob, kept for Mr Widdison's own use. He knotted the mane to serve for a handhold, backed the cob out of the stable, and turned his head downstream across the fields towards Swinbrook. The horse started and shied a little as he passed the old chapel, where a figure in Roman armour glowed faintly in the doorway, but he went the faster for that, and Dick saw to it that he set down his feet aright in the darkness. The household at Swinbrook Manor went to bed later than that at Widford, and there were lights still showing at an upper window and in the kitchen quarters. Reining in at the lighted window he saw three serving men and a boy playing at cards. He tapped on the window, and there was a startled pause. He tapped again.

'God be with us!' said one of the players. 'What's that? A hobgoblin?'

'It has a ghostly sound,' said another.

'Open the window,' said Dick in as manly a voice as he could produce. 'It is the letter, the letter my lady promised to send to the master's son. The old lady is no better, and we are anxious that it should go with tomorrow's messenger; so I rode with it at once.'

The rough catch of the window was turned with fumbling hands, and he thrust in the letter.

'Will you come in and take a glass of ale to keep out the cold?' said a voice with a tremor in it.

'It is late hours for us over there, I had best be gone,' said Hobberdy Dick. 'Another time maybe.'

He turned his horse, and it plunged away, so that the servant inside, who had snatched up a candle, could see no more than the flick of its tail. But the letter was in his hand, prosaic and substantial enough.

'No more than a roundhead servant with a merchant's screed,' he said. 'You had better mention it to my lady, Simon, when you take her packet tomorrow.'

Yet the four looked at each other palely, and shuffled their cards together, with no more heart to play.

Nine

When I a fat and bean-fed horse beguile,
Neighing in likeness of a filly foal.

A Midsummer Night's Dream

MR SILVESTER did not come the next day. He had
caught a cold in Stow churchyard and taken to his bed.
Mrs Widdison would still not allow that there was anything to alarm them in Mrs Dimbleby's condition; and
indeed there was little to lay hold on, except that her
voice had sunk to a thread of sound, and she never
moved unless she must.

Mr Widdison had little to do these days. Their
ploughing had been done at harvest time, and the
ground was too hard to dig. He sat in his office and
read over his accounts, and went up and down stairs
to visit his mother-in-law. He was increasingly uneasy
about her, but he let the day go by without sending
off his letter, for he was still expecting Mr Silvester.
That night the snow began to fall, steadily and without
cessation, so that by the morning the landscape was
already white. There was no wind, and it did not
blow into drifts, but it piled up all day, and Hobberdy
Dick shuffled uneasily through it, and peered out from
attic windows with a heavy heart. He peeped once or
twice into the old lady's room, and each time she
seemed to him further away. Unless Joel had made an
early start she would be gone before he arrived, and
Dick knew their hearts were set on a last meeting. At
length he thought of one thing that might keep her
for a little, though it meant a journey to Swinbrook

Farm, where there was a fine flock of geese. Early in the afternoon he set out through the smothering snow, which quickly covered his light footsteps. Humans, beasts and spirits seemed alike quieted by the snow, and not a soul was stirring. He moved in a small world of his own, which moved with him like a sphere. After a timeless while he drifted like a large snowflake into the whitened yard of Swinbrook Farm. Not a dropped feather was to be found, for they were all buried in snow. He climbed into the henhouse, where the drowsy hens stirred and cackled uneasily, and the remnant of geese who had survived that unfestive season, set up their shrill harsh cry. Dick did not want to be hunted by the farm dogs in mistake for a fox. He hastily collected a handful of feathers, and to make assurance sure plucked a couple from the fat gander, and made off down the hen ladder, leaving a clatter of protest behind him.

It was still light when he got back, the wind was rising, and Joel had not yet arrived. Inside it seemed already dusk. A noble fire was piled up in the hall, and Dick sat in the ingle nook and sorted his feathers, throwing the hens' feathers in the fire. He broke a piece of thread from the spinning wheel and tied the goose feathers into a small bundle, so that he could quickly find them again; then went upstairs to Mrs Dimbleby's room. Anne Seckar was there, supporting the old lady with one arm, while she fed her with sips of cordial posset. Dick made his way through the ardent haze, and crept under the bed. He tucked the bundle of feathers firmly into the crossed slats of the bed under the mattress, then darted back into the clearer air by the door, where he lingered, and peered wistfully at Mrs Dimbleby, wishing he could keep her by that means for good. But he knew it was futile. Once, hun-

85

dreds of years ago, when he was younger, he tried that method with a mortal who was dear to him; but all that he could keep by it had been her just-animate body upon the bed; and in the end he had plucked out the feathers, and let the straining spirit go. Indeed he was not even sure that the goose feathers would avail. Lapwings' would have been better if he could have found them, but the flocks of lapwings had gone down-stream, fearing the storm. If old Ursula had sense, too, she would lift the sick woman off the feather bed on to the floor when she began to be uneasy; but he did not much fear that, these townspeople knew so little.

Dick left the doorway soon, for he could not bear to watch the long hours of tossing that might follow if the summons came, and went up to the attic. He could see little through the drifting whirls of snow, but he sat there for some hours, sometimes watching, sometimes dozing lightly. He woke suddenly from a sleep of rather longer duration, and peered out sharply; for he seemed to see, or hear, or feel, the light of a dim and wavering lantern far downstream. He flung up the attic window, slithered with a cascade of snow down the roof and slid down a water-pipe. The wind was with him, though swirlingly, and blew him downstream. He had been right, the lantern was much further off than he could have seen, a couple of miles below Swinbrook, and on the far side of the river. It was a dim oil lantern, and Joel was holding it as low as he could, to prevent the fierce wind from blowing it out. With his other hand he gripped his horse's bridle, and rather suffered it to lead him than led it. Hobberdy Dick had time to think with approval how much Joel had gained in country ways since first they had met. He had the sense now to realize that his horse was his best guide, and to get onto terms with it. But Dick saw that Joel was already spent,

and that the horse had foundered. It would be a struggle for all three to get them safe home, and he would be glad to be spared the double plunge through running water. He gave a faint halloo, which seemed to Joel to come from far upstream. Joel answered it, with a sudden revival of hope, and cheered on the horse to a quicker pace. Thus they struggled on, one on each side of the river, till they came to the old ford below Swinbrook. Here Hobberdy Dick paused, and whinnied invitingly. At the same time the scent and appearance of a young mare hung on him for a moment. The horse, wearied though he was, responded bravely. He whinnied in return and plunged into the water, dragging Joel after him, all unprepared. In a moment the strong dark stream was round him, and, putting up his left hand to catch at the horse's mane, he lost his lantern, and was almost ready to despair, though his feet still felt the bottom. Dick whinnied again, and the horse floundered up the bank and came to him, with Joel still holding fast to bridle and rein. Dick spoke through the darkness.

'A stranger, sure enough,' he said. 'Where be you looking for, sir, this dark, stormy night?'

'I'm making for Widford Manor,' said Joel. 'Maybe I've strayed past it, for I'm sorely wandered.'

'No, no, sir, 'tis above you. We'm below Swinbrook yet. I be going that way myself, I be, though 'tis no night to be abroad in, and I'll see you to the door. They be in sad trouble, with the old lady ill and all.'

'I know,' said Joel. 'That's why I'm going in such haste. I should dearly love your company, but I can go but slowly, for my horse foundered and lost a shoe.'

'Never fear, sir,' said Dick. 'You hold to your horse, and he'll follow my mare, and us'll go so sweet and easy as may be.'

Again the horse was conscious of the scent and appearance of a young mare, and followed eagerly, so that it was all Joel could do to hold on and keep the pace against the bitter wind and snow. Indeed Hobberdy Dick himself found it hard enough going. It was no time for talking, and they moved on by fits, as the horse slackened and quickened his pace. It seemed to Joel that they moved on for ever; but, considering the conditions, they made good way, and were knocking at the great door soon after ten o'clock.

'Come in, sir, and spend the night,' said Joel. 'It is no weather to be going further.' But he spoke to the drifting snow; for as he loosed the rein to knock, Dick had led the horse round to the stable, and hammered there till George Batchford came down. Then the horse pushed in, and walked with hanging head and trailing rein to an empty stall, as if he knew the stable, though he was a stranger.

In the meantime, at Joel's knocking, lights went up in the darkened house. Mr Widdison, who had been sitting at Mrs Dimbleby's bedside, came down to open the door, and Joel staggered in, dripping from the river and whitened with snow.

'Is Gran still alive?' he said.

'Joel!' said his father; and then, 'She is still alive, though she is sinking, and longs to see you. But how is it that you're here?'

'I set out as soon as I got your letter. I felt that she was more ill than you knew, and that I must come at once.'

By this time they had been joined by most of the household, variously attired, and Mrs Widdison said sharply: 'Well, since he is come, you'd better get him something dry to wear and something warm to eat, or he'll get his death. Maria, blow up the fire and heat up something for him; Charity, fetch your master's cloak which is drying in front of the fire.'

'I must see to my horse,' said Joel. 'It went round towards the stable.'

'Ned,' said Mr Widdison, 'go and wake George Batchford, and tell him to look to it. Go down to the kitchen, Joel, and change there. The girls will bring you your things, and it is warmest there. But be quick.'

The household bustled round Joel, fetching him clothes and forcing a hot drink upon him; but Mr Widdison stood in the hall, pondering.

'My letter!' he said. 'I never sent it.'

He went into the office and unlocked his box. The letter was not there and though he dropped candle-grease over his papers searching for it, it was not to be found.

In the meantime Joel, with hasty and fumbling fingers, had pulled on a suit of his own, which had been left behind in the Autumn, and then, after swallowing a half-warmed draught of milk, had gone upstairs, too intent upon being in time to notice how over-wearied he was. The rest fell back when he came to the door, and he went into the room alone. There was only one person with his grandmother – if we except Hobberdy Dick, who was crouching under the bed ready to pluck out the goose feathers when Joel came. She was a young girl, whose pale gold hair was caught by the candle-light as she knelt to support Mrs Dimbleby.

'He is come, madam,' she said tenderly. 'That is granted you too.'

'Goodness and mercy have surely –' whispered Mrs Dimbleby, and the thread of sound died away as her eyes and Joel's leapt together. Joel stood for a long moment in the doorway, and content passed and repassed between them. Then he went to the bed, and Anne relinquished the light weight to him, and left the room. Dick plucked out the goose feathers and followed her, for he felt in his heart that the conversation between them, however shortened, must owe nothing to magic. As he went the fever left the old woman's blood, and with it some of her strength, so that to those clustered round the door it seemed that only her lips moved. But Joel, with his ear to her mouth, heard her, and replied almost as low, so that for five precious minutes they talked together in a kind of solitude. Then the weeping women in the doorway were joined by Samuel Widdison, and gradually followed him into the room. There was half an hour of silence; at the end of it Charity tiptoed over to the window and opened it. Mrs Dimbleby said suddenly in a stronger voice:

'Lift me, my dear. The Lord bless you, Samuel, for your kindness to me and your dear love to my Nan. Forgive me, all of you, the times I have troubled you or done you wrong. Where is the little mistress?' Mrs Widdison came forward.

'Not you, my dear, though I thank you too; but the little mistress who has ministered to me, so like my Nan.' Charity ran to fetch Anne from the attic where she was praying, but before she could come Mrs Dimbleby said, 'Thank her for me, Joel. I can't wait. Lay me down and cross my hands.'

He laid her down, and crossed her leaden hands on her breast. She shut her eyes; and before Anne came down from her attic she was beyond their reach.

Ten

For that unworthy guest so senseless is
And deaf, no exorcist can make him hear.

HENRY MORE, *The Praeexistencie of the Soul*

UNTIL Mrs Dimbleby died the household did not
know how large a place she filled in it. Even in the
torpor of her illness her presence had pervaded the
house, and on the morning after her death everyone
moved about as if stunned. Mrs Widdison wept
honestly and copiously; yet below her tears she alone
felt a faint stirring of relief, a sense of liberty from
some unacknowledged restraint.

Joel was worn out and fevered after his long struggle
through the snow, and yet curiously at peace. The
wind had fallen, the snow was drifted high about the
house, and within and without everything was muffled
into an almost unnatural silence. In that Puritan and
city household few rites were observed. George Batchford brought in sprigs of yew to stick in the shroud,
Anne set salt upon the coffin, but the candles she put
round it were not allowed, and she alone watched it on
the first night.

Joel had gone to bed early, still numbed and peace-
ful, and had fallen into a heavy sleep. He awaked
from it in the small hours, and was suddenly invaded
by desolation. The only mother he had known was
gone from him, the only tenderness that had ever
been bestowed on him had retreated and left him to
loneliness. His grief would not let him rest, and he
flung on some clothes, and went to the room where his

grandmother still lay. As he opened the door he saw
that the room did not depend entirely for light on the
bedroom rush which he carried. Another like it was
set on the chest, and seated on the hard-backed chair
with her hands folded was the pale girl whom he had
seen when he last came to that room, and to whom his
grandmother had sent a message of thanks and farewell. The whole scene, which he had not noticed at the
time, came back as vividly as if it was before his eyes.
He could look from detail to detail and observe it,
though then he had only seen his grandmother. The
girl raised her head, and they looked gravely and
steadily at each other. Dick from a dark corner observed with pleasure the meeting of the two people
whom he loved in the house.

'I don't think I quite know who you are,' said Joel
at length. 'My grandmother called you the young mistress, and sent her thanks to you.'

'It's I who owe her thanks,' said Anne. 'I am Anne
Seckar, and Mrs Widdison's waiting gentlewoman.'

'I had heard that my mother-in-law had one, but
nothing of her,' said Joel. 'I can hardly believe that you
are she.'

'Are you come to watch?' said Anne. 'I will leave you
then. For, though Charity will watch tomorrow night if
I am with her, she dare not sit here alone.'

'There is no need for you to watch,' said Joel. 'She
is not here.'

'No, I know,' said Anne. 'No-one ever went more
swiftly when once she was loosed. But it is our custom
round here to watch the body to show our love and
duty.'

'You must be tired, for I am sure you have been
nursing her, and waking late,' said Joel. 'I will watch
the rest of tonight, if you think it should be done.'

'But you had that long struggle through the snow.'

'I couldn't sleep anyway; that's why I came here.'

'Very well, I will go,' said Anne, who had a day's work ahead of her. She gathered up the blanket which had been wrapped round her, but on second thought offered it to Joel.

'I'll get my own,' he said. 'I'm sure you need that if you sleep in the attics. As I suppose you do,' he added shyly. He fetched his blanket. Anne wished him a good night, curtsied and went. Joel and Hobberdy Dick were left alone with the lovely and outworn body; but Joel was no longer quite so desolate.

The snow still lay thick round the house on the day of the funeral; but a path had been dug through the fields to Swinbrook, and the coffin was carried there without pomp. There were few outside mourners; but Lady Fettiplace sent one of her running footmen to mark her respect. Mrs Widdison was deeply gratified when she heard of it.

'A very proper attention,' she said to her husband, when Mr Silvester and the preachers had eaten their cake and gone. 'It shows that Lady Fettiplace knows what is due to us. It is only old Madam who is so rude and overbearing, and she is the same to all.'

'Lady Fettiplace had a great liking to my mother-in-law,' said Samuel Widdison, and went to find Joel. He found him, coughing and feverish on the settle in the hall.

'Sit down, boy,' he said kindly, as Joel got to his feet. 'I fear you've not recovered from that night of storm. I have not heard of your ride yet. Have you the letter that summoned you?'

Joel took it from his pocket book and his father studied it.

'That is the letter I writ you,' he said at last. 'But, Joel, I never sent it. Who brought it you?'

'One of the Lady Fettiplace's men.'

'My Lady Fettiplace offered to send a letter for me, and I wrote one, but locked it in my desk. The night you came I looked in the desk for it, it was gone; but the lock was untampered with, and my key had never left my bunch.'

'It is beyond understanding,' said Joel, 'for I had strange help on the way, or I should not have got here in time.'

'I have not yet heard of your journey.'

'It was not snowing when I left London, but by the time I got to Oxford it was snowing hard. Before Minster my horse fell and lost a shoe; but I could not find another at Minster, so I borrowed a lantern and went on on foot, taking my horse as a guide, because they said it was much stormier upstream. And so it was, and I could hardly make my way. Then a man hailed me across the river, and my horse plunged across. He said he was going beyond Widford, and would see me there. So we went on together. And when we got to the door I asked him to come in and spend the night – but there was no one there.'

'Perhaps he had gone on, and in the strong wind you never noticed his parting,' said Mr Widdison. 'But this is a strange place – strange and not altogether good.'

'But mainly good,' said Joel eagerly. 'Sir, I love this house and everything about it, and would live here always if I might.'

Mr Widdison made no reply, and they fell into silence. At length Mr Widdison got up.

'Well, there is no moving while the snow is so deep. You must nurse your cold, and make the most of your time while you are here. Tomorrow you shall make me your report of how things go on Cheapside.'

He moved away, and a sigh of disappointment broke

from Joel, echoed in the shadows by Hobberdy Dick.
Each felt that he had made an effort that deserved a
better return. Joel had never spoken to his father so
frankly of his desires, and Hobberdy Dick had been
sure that now Joel was brought home by great exertion
he would be allowed to stay. There seemed to be a
strange pull about this unknown Cheapside, which
drew men there almost against their will. Dick knew
no one who could tell him about it, except perhaps
the miser's ghost in the bed. He resolved to have a
conversation with it, if the poor shadowy thing had
still power to converse. With this purpose in mind he
went down to the best bedroom that night, after he had
seen Anne fall into a wearied slumber. He expected
Mr and Mrs Widdison to be asleep too, but they were
awake later than usual. They were talking, and about
something that concerned Hobberdy Dick.

'But you know,' Mrs Widdison was saying, 'that
her little jointure would be long ago spent on her
keep.'

'That depends,' said Mr Widdison, 'upon what part
of the business you counted it as invested in. If it had
gone to buy the Cathay silks it would have brought a
handsome return, enough to send the boy to College.'

'Now Samuel, that's soft,' said his wife. 'Why count
it was invested in the most paying part of the business,
when you know quite well that's taking the bread out
of your children's mouths, just to further the old lady's
whim of sending her grandson to College.'

'After all Joel's my own eldest son,' said Mr Widdison, stung. 'If my money can't send him to College,
whose can?'

'As your eldest son he'll have a right to the business,'
said Mrs Widdison, rising on her elbow. 'What's the
use of training him to think himself above it? He's too

ready to do that now. All that he really wants is to idle about in the country, making friends with all the riotous young cavaliers that he meets. It will be time enough to think of College when Samuel is of the age for it. Things will have settled down by then after the War, and we shall know where we are and what we can afford.'

'I didn't notice all this talk about affording when you were buying your carriage and the new furnishings for the house,' said Mr Widdison. 'None the less,' he added, 'there is something in what you say.'

Mrs Widdison opened her mouth to answer him, but was seized by a severe cramp in the left foot, and bent herself hastily, with an exclamation of pain, to rub it.

'I'm sure this house is damp,' she said. 'I never had these pains in Cheapside. I wish you'd have it seen to. In that mild spell before Christmas the walls were running.'

'All Cotswold houses are the same, I understand,' said Mr Widdison. 'If you live in the country you cannot expect the comforts of London. And at least there is no fear of the plague.'

The conversation died out at this, and they turned away from each other, but it was some time before either slept. The ghost muttered, and searched about among the clothes. At length one low snore answered another, and Hobberdy Dick swarmed up and perched on the footrail of the bed.

'Tell us, Gaffer,' he said, 'what do they do in this Cheapside o' their'n?'

'Out of reckoning,' said the ghost. 'Out of reckoning! There's one angel lost for a surety.'

'Can't 'ee answer a civil question?' said Dick exasperated. 'I want a tell with 'ee.'

97

'Three and five make eight,' said the ghost, starting his counting over again, 'and two ten.'

'What do they do in Cheapside?' said Dick doggedly.

'Ten and twenty, thirty, and twenty, fifty,' said the ghost. 'That pile's all square.'

Dick stretched out a lean hand, and grasped one of the ghost's visionary money bags.

'Can't 'ee talk sense?' he said. 'I'll keep this till ye give me a fair answer.'

The stuff of the bag clung to his fingers like a sticky cobweb and made his flesh creep a little, but he whipped it away resolutely. The ghost broke into a high keening wail, and scrabbled frantically among the bedclothes. Mr Widdison woke with a yell, and wakened Mrs Widdison.

'Whatever is the matter?' she cried. 'Yelling out like that! It's enough to frighten one to death.'

'I'm all of a sweat,' said Mr Widdison. 'I dreamt thieves were breaking into the strong box at the shop, and carrying off every bit of silver we had in the house. I saw them as plain as day. There was one lean fellow in rags, and a fat white one somewhere behind; and they'd knocked old Ursula on the head, and she was screaming like a peacock. I don't call to mind that I've ever had such a clear dream in my life. I hope it forebodes nothing.'

'A chill most likely,' said his wife. 'Maybe you've caught Joel's cold.'

'I daresay you're right. I'm shaking still, and the sheets strike deadly chill. I'll go down and get myself a glass of hot rhenish.'

'I'll get it for you,' said Mrs Widdison, who, sleepy as she was, knew her wifely duties. 'If you've a cold starting it's the worst thing in the world to go down through these draughty passages.'

She fumbled with sleepy fingers at the flint, and at length took a taper, and went down in the dark to light it at the embers of the fire. Mr Widdison stayed unwillingly in the dark, for the ghost was searching frantically among the bedclothes, and causing a most unpleasant draught in the bed. Dick felt it was not the time for conversation. He pushed back a forgotten panel in the wainscotting, freed his hand from the clinging bag, which he left there; and before Mrs Widdison had come back with her mulled wine and lighted taper he was down in the stable among the horses.

Eleven

By Night affrighted, in his fearfull Dreames,
Of raging Fiends and Goblins that he meets.

DRAYTON, *The Barons Warres*

FOR three nights Dick tried to get some coherent
description out of the ghost by dangling the money bag
in front of it, and promising its return if the ghost
would give him any useful information; but it was
really clear to him from the first that the attempt
was hopeless. The poor thing disintegrated still more
under the effect of its loss, and could only wail and
clutch about. It hardly even seemed able to see Dick,
and only vaguely to apprehend the presence of the
money bag which he dangled in front of it. On the
third night he gave up the attempt, peeled the decom-
posing, sticky thing off his hand with relief, and threw
it back to the ghost, who crooned over it brokenly,
and fell to counting its money again with accents less
distinct than before.

Those three nights had been a trying experience
for Mr Widdison. He had found it difficult to get to
sleep in the disturbed and draughty bed, and when he
slept he was wakened again and again by dreams of
loss, less distinct than the first night's, but always of
loss, by fire, pillage or monstrous negligence in the
shop. After the third night he said to his wife:

'These things must have a signification, and be sent
me for a warning. It would be wrong to neglect them.
It is clear I must go up to town and see to the business
myself. Who knows what that boy has let slide through

inexperience? Maybe one of the clerks has yielded to temptation, and is falsifying the books. It is clear that a master's eye is needed.'

'Fancy making your way up to London through all this snow, just for a few nights' dreams!' said Mrs Widdison. 'And when you have these chills too. 'Tis not safe. Do stay, Samuel. Send Joel if someone must go.'

'I tell you it's of no use to send Joel,' said Samuel Widdison. 'The boy is honest and hard-working, but how can he judge of what's best to do in an emergency, or what's going wrong with the business? There's more in these dreams and tokens than we used to reckon for. As for the snow, it's still lying, but the ways are getting trodden now, and I had best get away before more falls. Pack my saddle bags, and I will set out betimes. Jonathon Fletcher shall go with me as far as Oxford. Cheer up, my mouse, and if all goes well I'll send you a pretty fairing home from Cheapside.'

Mrs Widdison much disliked his going. She felt shorn of her consequence without her husband's support, and she feared that Joel would gain too much authority as son of the house. She was anxious as well about her husband's health; for these night-time chills in a bed which felt warm to her seemed ominous of a decline. But though she wept and begged him to stay Mr Widdison was determined to go; so there was nothing for it but to set about the preparations as quickly as possible. In the meantime Mr Widdison went to give his instructions to Joel and to George Batchford, which he did before the household met for prayers.

Joel was still dressing when his father called him from the closet under the stairs, and he came out tying his points, with the belt which concealed them over his arm.

'Come into my office, boy,' said Samuel Widdison. 'Have you noticed that any about the shop are loose in their ways, or apt to go astray?'

'I have sometimes thought,' said Joel, 'that some of the journeymen were ready to take advantage of me, and stay long on their errands; but I had rather not tell you which, for Job Baker and I dealt with them, and I don't want to seem a tale-bearer.'

'And you kept an eye over Job Baker himself? For you must know that the honestest servant and the oldest may be tempted by his master's absence, and fall from his good ways. We have Scripture warrant for it.'

'Oh no, Father, I am sure old Job is honest, but perhaps over-strict to deal with the prentices. Surely you have no reason to suspect him?'

'No, I have no special reason. But – I tell you this in your ear, Joel, and it is not to get abroad – these three nights I have had dreams of heavy loss, such as it seems rash to neglect, and it struck me that the loss might rather be from the dishonesty of my servants than from open calamity, and therefore might the more call for my presence.'

'You know, Father, that I have had short experience of the work because of my schooling. I tried my best to oversee things, but I may well have missed what you would have noticed.'

'You have been a good son to me, Joel, and done your work to the best of your ability; but I think it is time for me to go back to the shop. I show my confidence by leaving you in charge here. You shall have it in hand to pay the men's wages and oversee their work. Do not allow George Batchford to think himself the master in the farm. Check him sometimes, no matter though he be in the right. Here are the keys of the strong box, and give out the money to your mother-in-law for the expenses of the house. I will leave her so much as to serve for a week. And if she desires any extraordinary expense write to me for permission. And look you keep sober company, and do not fall into idle ways. I daresay we shall soon change places, but in the meantime God keep you, and preserve you constant to your charge.'

'I will do my best, sir, God helping me,' said Joel. Mr Widdison went out to speak to George Batchford, and Joel back to his room to finish dressing.

Hobberdy Dick had been busy digging up grubs for the birds in the pile of leaves at the back of the Summer House, and had heard nothing of this unexpected success. He found a bustle in the yard when he came in, after dividing his finds between the tits and the thrushes. At first he thought Joel was being packed off, and was angry; but the preparations seemed too extensive for that. He went indoors and found the family at breakfast, with special fortifications of ham and raised pie for Mr Widdison: but it was not until he heard Mr and Mrs Widdison's parting speeches as the saddle bags were being strapped that he realized how well the ghost had served him after all. He wished in compunctious gratitude that he could send it back to Cheapside behind Mr Widdison, where its native air might restore it; but it was too frail for that, and it would be unkind to saddle Mr Widdison with such a travelling companion. Hobberdy Dick went out to see if the frost still held, for a sudden thaw would make the road dangerous; but to his relief it promised to hold for several days. He watched with approval while Mr Widdison blessed his children, spoke some parting words aside to Joel, and mounted his horse, whom Dick had sleeked down into a good temper with grooming and flattery and some choice wisps of hay. He watched the two men out of sight from the bare branches of his oak tree, and enjoyed a short nap in the bright winter sun. Then he stretched himself.

'No time for idling, Dick,' he said to himself. 'Us has our work cut out now, to make the place prosper.'

Twelve

Thomalin, why sitten we soe,
As weren overwent with woe,
    Upon so fayre a morow?
The joyous time now nigheth fast,
That shall alegge this bitter blast,
    And slake the winters sorowe.

SPENSER, *The Shepheardes Calendar*

THE snow continued to lie for several weeks, so that
there was little to be done about the farm. Mrs Widdison's temper was much fretted by the confinement, and
by the authority which Mr Widdison had given to Joel.
She thought that the key of the strong box should have
been given to her, and felt it a monstrous invasion of
her privileges that a boy of eighteen should be em-
powered to pay the men, and even to limit her
expenses. It was the worse since there seemed little
prospect of her husband's return, for he wrote to Joel
that the event had fully justified his going. The ill-will
between the Army and the Parliament had risen to
such a pitch that all sober men feared for disturbances
– the town was crammed with ranting Fifth Monarchy
men, who respected no private property; and it was on
all counts necessary that a master's eye should oversee
the business.

Joel, on his side, wrote his father careful weekly
accounts of all that was done in the place, enclosing
copies of any bills that had to be paid. There was little
of farm work, however, to occupy his time, and the
keen frost gave them an opportunity for winter sports.

The flooded land across the Windrush was frozen

solid; and Joel learned to skate, and he and Ned pushed the little girls on chairs over the ice. They built a great snow house in the meadows with the help of some of the Swinbrook boys, and held and besieged it with snowballs; they made rough sledges and slid down the snowy hills.

Hobberdy Dick had to content himself with these outdoor sports, for the fireside merriment which he liked best was impeded by the ill-humour of Ursula in the kitchen and Mrs Widdison in the parlour. Nothing very riotous would have been thought of at that time of mourning, when the loss of Mrs Dimbleby hung over the house; but there might have been room for old tales and songs, and gentle mirth. The maids span diligently in the kitchen, driven on by old Ursula's tongue, and the little girls struggled with their embroidery in the Drawing-Room, not without tears. Joel took out his small store of books, and tried to keep up his Latin and mathematics, struggling against the drowsiness brought on by hours outside in the keen frosty air.

So things went on till the last week in February, when the thaw came, and the Windrush spread over the lower fields, and Joel brought in hazel catkins from the woods, which no-one valued but Martha and Anne Seckar. These wintry weeks had been the hardest on Anne. It was bad enough for the little girls; but they could sometimes beg time off from their lessons, to play on the ice, or snowball out of sight of the Drawing-Room windows. But Mrs Widdison grew more exacting with boredom, and Anne had hard work to think of ways of entertaining her. She had introduced her to the padded silk work which had been fashionable ten years back, and was still a genteel novelty to Mrs Widdison. But she could not draw well enough to do the designs, which fell to Anne, and only cared to do the more amusing part of the fancy work; so that Anne had to spend her odd moments of spare time working over the dull patches. Still, between them they worked a cover to a jewel box, which the Swinbrook carpenter made to Anne's design. With this and with the never-ending care of Mrs Widdison's clothes, with household work and with the making of cakes and confections, and the children's lessons Anne was busy from morning to night. Here Joel could do nothing; he had no power over his stepmother's maids, and his influence with her was less than nothing. He was not, however, the less concerned.

Next to Joel Anne missed Mrs Dimbleby most of all. The children missed her suddenly and intolerably when they were in trouble, Martha the most of them; but Martha found some consolation in the baby, whom she was teaching to stand and talk. Little Samuel ran after Joel, and went about by preference on his shoulders. His mother saw little of him in consequence, for Joel avoided his stepmother as much as possible because when she spoke to him she was rarely civil.

In spite of fretted tempers the appearance of the house was prosperous. The best bedroom was free of rats, the furniture shone with polish, the fires glowed brightly, the livestock and poultry prospered, nothing was lost or mislaid, the corn and hay lasted well and the autumn pullets started to lay early. Foxes robbed some of the neighbouring hen-roosts, but none came to Widford. Except for winter colds and chilblains everyone was well but Mrs Widdison and old Ursula, who suffered from frequent cramps and curious little bruisings of their legs, which looked like the mark of fingernails. Neither noticed that this affliction came on after bouts of scolding and ill-temper.

The winter frost and then the floods closed the little household in, so that the weekly pilgrimage to church was quite an event. It was not till the middle of March that they received a visit, and that was from their nearest neighbour, Lady Fettiplace. Mrs Widdison's ill-humour melted like a snow wreath at the sight of the coach, and she was all joyous bustle. Lady Fettiplace came without her mother-in-law, for old Madam Fettiplace was spending the day in her Burford dower house, where she was to be installed as soon as the Spring had fairly come. The visit was the easier for her absence. Lady Fettiplace asked to see the children and played with the baby, and praised Anne's singing. She much admired the embroidered box which had just been sent home, and on hearing that Anne had designed it asked diffidently if she could be spared for a day to show her how to set about the design for an old chest which she wished to re-cover. She added, 'Madam Fettiplace will be leaving me soon, and I shall be alone in the house, for my uncle keeps to his room. I should be glad if you, madam, would come over sometimes and spend the day with me, if you can bring yourself to leave all your family and occupations here.'

'Oh my lady, I should be too much honoured, and of course I will send my gentlewoman over as often as your ladyship desires. I hope she will make herself useful.'

'Thank you. Shall we say next Tuesday?'

Lady Fettiplace consented to take more wine and biscuits, but excused herself from staying to dinner because she had to dine with Madam Fettiplace in Burford, and fetch her home before dusk. She took her leave and went, leaving good humour behind her. Mrs Widdison was too happy to resist making a confidante of Anne.

'I told my husband how it would be. It is old Madam Fettiplace who is so high and ill-humoured. As soon as she is gone my lady will be perfectly ready to be neighbourly. You saw how she was, all affability and condescension.'

'Yes, I think she is very gentle and obliging,' said Anne.

'We mustn't let you neglect your singing,' said Mrs Widdison. 'Have you some new songs you wish to learn? You had better practise them this evening; I will tell Ursula to see that the maids do the mending tonight. They have nothing to do down there in the kitchen.'

This good humour lasted for several days, and Mrs Widdison's night cramps did not trouble her at all. Old Ursula, on the other hand, suffered dreadfully.

On Tuesday morning Anne was bustled off betimes to Swinbrook Manor, and spent a long day there. On her return Mrs Widdison was eager to question her about the household, and pleased to hear that Lady Fettiplace had but one gentlewoman. Anne patiently gave particulars of what they ate, and the plenishings of the house and table, but gave vague answers to more intimate questions; and at length Mrs Widdison dismissed her to the work which had accumulated for her during the day. It was late before she went to bed.

Next morning Anne was busy in the outer kitchen with some fine ironing which Ursula would not trust to the maids when Joel came through to take off his muddy boots by the fire.

'We have sown all the upper fields now,' he said. 'I hope it's dry enough. It's a bad thing to have no experience; but George Batchford thinks it is dry enough.' He came over in his stockinged feet to watch her. 'Did you enjoy yourself yesterday? It must be rest for you to be among your equals again.'

She looked up with a sudden flooding of colour to her cheeks, and the blue of her eyes deepened with unshed tears.

'It is quick of you to know,' she said. 'I hope I have not seemed proud and strange.'

'Not proud, but most strange, and lovely,' said Joel haltingly. 'It is as if you had come from another world from us, like my grandmother's tale of the fairy bride. And yet,' he added musingly, 'I suppose it is the other way round. It's we who come from the other world, and all this belongs to you. Gran called you the little mistress, and it was always true what she spoke.'

Anne took the cooling iron back to the fire, and fetched a hot one.

'The house feels empty without her,' she said. 'Yet she was so glad to go that we couldn't grudge it her. But it seemed always when she was there that there was a protection against the worst things.'

'So there is still if we could but feel it,' said Joel. 'But it all seems very bare without her. The Lady Fettiplace came to get leave to have you, didn't she?'

'Yes, your grandmother told her about me and that we were distantly akin, and she thought that I might be her friend. She is lonely, poor lady, when her husband is away, and a little fearful about the birth of her child. The old gentleman, his uncle, is broken and quiet, and has never got over the King's death. But I think it will be better for her in some ways when Madam Fettiplace is gone.'

Old Ursula came in, driving Charity in front of her, and Joel put on his slippers and went.

Thirteen

Hicketty Picketty, my red hen,
She lays eggs for gentlemen;
Sometimes nine, sometimes ten;
Hicketty Picketty, my red hen.

IT was a fine April day towards the end of Lent. There
had been little fasting that Lent in Puritan Burford,
nor in the household at Widford. No pancakes had
been tossed on Shrove Tuesday, and eggs had been
eaten as plentifully after it as before it. The eggs at
Widford, however, had been scarcer during Lent.
Hobberdy Dick cared little for Christian fasts, but he
deeply resented the breaking of the annual truce between man and the warm-blooded kinds which per-
mitted of the safe rearing of eggs and young. He had
incited the hens to lay out, and helped to hide their
nests and mislead the searchers. His own hen was too
feather-pated, and too much puffed-up by her un-
deserved eminence to make a good sitter. She would
lay a clutch, cluck aimlessly for a week or so, and start
laying in a new place. Dick distributed her deserted
eggs among the more assiduous mothers.

On this Tuesday in Holy Week, Mrs Widdison had
wrenched the horses away from the farm work, and
gone out in the coach for a day's visiting. She had taken
Anne with her to accompany her on the drive, and sit
in the coach while she paid her visits. Since Lady
Fettiplace had made friends with Anne Mrs Widdison
had begun to have hopes of social success. Lady Fettiplace well understood on what conditions the friendship would be allowed; and she had not only invited

Mrs Widdison to dine with her at Swinbrook, but had persuaded one of her Wenman cousins to visit at Widford. It was to return this call, and to visit the Silvesters at Burford, that Mrs Widdiford set out, dressed with anxious care and in a flutter of spirits. Martha took the opportunity to slip out to the woods with Samuel, to look for primroses.

It was a soft, sunny spring day, with a tumbling wind. The fields were deep in mud, and the woods smelt of spring earth and flowers, and the sap of trees. The glades were white with wood anemones, and there were rarer clumps of wood-sorrel, and scattered bunches of primroses. In the drier places the first of the ground ivy began to show patches of bright blue-purple. Samuel shouted and rolled about among the flowers, muddying himself recklessly, and Martha ran from clump to clump, picking carefully and with long stems where she thought a blossom could be spared, for she loved growing things. They were not alone in the wood. A little group of Fulbrook children were picking there too, who had played truant like Martha; but they had escaped from the serious work of glove-making, and she only from the leisure of lessons. There was a motherly little girl of nine, and two smaller children of six and seven, and a toddler rather older than Samuel. Thanks to George Batchford, Martha had by now a tolerable command of good Oxfordshire, and need no longer be afraid of accosting the children. She and the eldest girl, Marion Barnard, were soon sitting together, bunching their flowers and tying them up with long grasses.

''Tis not long to May Day now,' said Marion, 'and so flowery a May Day as us could wish, though 'twon't be like the old days. My Grannie says as how when her was a girl, aye and when my Mammie was a girl too, they had a great old dragon carried through Burford streets, all painted gold and red, and there was guisers and morris men dancing behind it, all in green and yellow and white, and they set up the maypole on Church Green, and danced round it like David in front of the Ark.'

'And what do you do now?'

'If we get out to Wychwood to gather wild flowers and make a grotto 'tis as much as we can do,' said Marion. 'For my dad takes the strap to we if a catches we out o' night. But on May night Mammie don't let on to 'un. But 'tis Easter morning before May Day. That's the best day that comes before May Day, so 'tis.'

'What do 'ee do Easter morning?' said Martha. 'Us be from the city, where they don't know aught of country ways.'

'Why, Easter day, that's the day the sun dances, if so be as 'tis fine enough to see it. And on Easter Saturday us boils eggs hard in saffron or green nettles or the like, and us goes up Fulbrook Hill before sunrise, and us rolls the eggs down; and her whose egg rolls the furthest and straightest, why 'tis good luck for she the whole year, so 'tis.'

'Can I come too?' said Martha.

'Come and welcome,' said Marion. 'Old and young'll be rolling their eggs on Easter Sunday; but don't let the ministers know, nor yet the godly, for they do cut up terrible rough about Easter and all the Saints' days. My daddy he be one of the godly, and we have a power of them down to our house, and they do talk like a book about Hell-fire and all. I dearly love to hear them, but little Keren there is main frittened.'

Here they were interrupted by a raid from a small gang of boys who were birds' nesting near. Marion would have made no resistance, merely sheltered her little sisters behind her, and wept at the pelting of mud and oak-apples, but Martha was more bellicose; she doubled her fists and sallied out against them. It might have gone hard with her, for though the boys were not big they were rough, and annoyed at a resistance to which they were not accustomed; but as they charged in a yelling bunch the first unaccountably tripped on a stick in his way. The stick shot up and entangled itself in the legs of the second, and the remaining three tumbled over them in a confused heap into a deeper and stickier mud than they had reckoned on. They turned to cuff each other, and Marion signed to Martha to steal away. Martha picked up her nosegays and moved away composedly.

'That was our little man,' she said when she joined Marion.

'Hobberdy Dick?' said Marion, whispering.

'I don't know his name,' said Martha. 'He's a little ragged man that does things about the house. I see him sometimes.'

Marion looked at her with awe.

'Thee belongs to Widford right enough,' she said. 'The boys'll never touch thee if they know Hobberdy Dick has a mind to thee. I reckon thee can go about the woods where thee will.'

But she drew away from Martha with something like awe, and they parted soon afterwards.

Martha went home thinking of Easter Sunday, and how to make herself an Easter egg. This proved a more difficult matter than she had expected, for, not wishing to get Charity into trouble, she applied to old Ursula, who disapproved of the whole business from beginning to end.

'Eggs?' she said. 'And what do you want eggs for?'

'For to make coloured ones for me and Samuel,' said Martha.

'Against Easter Sunday, I suppose,' said old Ursula. 'Do you think I'll give you eggs, and so scarce as they are too, to go boiling them up with your heathen mummeries and witcheries, and rolling them down the hill on Easter morning like an own sister to the Scarlet Woman? Be off with you out of here, and if Charity gives you so much as an egg I'll speak to the mistress, and back she can go to the charity what reared her, and a good riddance too.'

'What's all the screeching for?' said George Batchford, coming in with the empty pig pails.

'Keep your long tongue out of this,' said Ursula, 'and your dirty feet off my clean floor that the girl's just free-stoned. And if you think that pig pail's washed you can think again.'

'Then wash it yourself,' said George, 'since you're so choice.' He and Martha went out together.

'Ursula!' said George Batchford. 'I've heard tell 'tis Greek for she-bear. I wish I had the baiting of her, though 'twould be a powerful fierce dog would get the better of she. What was she a letting forth for?'

'I asked her for some eggs to boil up against Sunday,' said Martha. 'I main wanted to roll them down Fulbrook Hill with the rest.'

'So you should, for 'twill bring good luck to the place. Charity will give you an egg or two and welcome.'

'I dursn't ask her,' said Martha, 'for Ursula says she'll have her turned away if she gives me one; she would too, she has a spite against Charity.'

'Who's to know if Charity does?'

'She might ask me, and it goes against me to tell lies.'

'Seems to me,' said George Batchford, 'that those as

116

ask what they oughtn't may look to be told what isn't. Still, maybe you can't frame your tongue to one. Pity, for you could boil them up in an old pot over the saddleroom fire, and none would be any the wiser. But we could ill spare Charity.'

George had been raking muck as he spoke, and Martha had been swinging to and fro by the catch of the Barn door. Now she suddenly let go, for she heard a distant cackling in the copse across the yard.

'What a fool I be, George,' she said. 'There's a hen laying out. If I can find her egg I'll never need to ask Charity,' and she ran across the lane and into the copse.

The cackling was further off than she thought; she had to cross the stream, and even when it sounded quite near she could see no hen. When she seemed close to it it stopped, and for a short time she hunted around in vain. Then under a pile of brushwood she came on a scooped-out nest filled with neat brown eggs, not very large.

'Ten,' said Martha, counting them. 'One for Samuel and one for me, one for Rachel and one for George, one for Charity and one for Anne, one for Joel and one for Ned, and two for Charity's basket.'

She gathered the eggs into her apron and fetched a compass round the house, humming below her breath:

> Hicketty Picketty, my red hen,
> She lays eggs for gentlemen,

and behind her the song was taken up, even lower:

> Sometimes nine, sometimes ten,
> Hicketty Picketty, my red hen.

Fourteen

The first they met was old Carl Hood.
He's aye for ill and never for good.

The Ballad of Earl Brand

IT was a happy party that climbed the hill above Widford and made for the Fulbrook road early on Easter Sunday. Hobberdy Dick followed them, though at a distance, for there was always something a little frightening about Easter; strange presences were abroad, and alien footsteps brushed the dew.

It was very still, in the hush that goes before the second bird song at dawn. George and Joel carried lanterns, Samuel pattered beside Joel or rode on his shoulder, as the whim took him. When they were at a safe distance from the house George Batchford raised the Pace Egg song. Only Anne knew it of their party, but the song was taken up by a small group that came straggling up from Swinbrook way. It was surprising to see the number who came to the egg-rolling in that Puritan district; most households of any size had some representatives. When they dipped down into Fulbrook quite a crowd joined them. They walked cautiously through Fulbrook, for the godly were asleep there, and no one wished to waken them. Dick skirted the village, and made directly for the smooth slope of Fulbrook Hill. He crouched in a gorse bush, and waited for the pace-eggers to come up. His party was among the first, Martha and Rachel walking ahead with Marion Barnard and some of the Fulbrook children. As they climbed the hill Marion gave a start, and peered into the dusk.

'There's old Mother Darke,' she said. 'What's her doing here for the egg-rolling? Spit on your palm and rub the egg with it, or she'll be ill-wishing us.'

Martha did as she was told, and saw a dark figure under a hawthorn bush at a little distance to their left. She did not accost anyone, only stood motionless watching them; but more than one started as he passed her, and spat into his fist. It was not usual for the witches to come to the Easter egg-rolling. At the top of the hill, however, most of them seemed to forget her, and they waited, with song and laughter and some mock bickering among the children, while the light strengthened. The little girls laid their eggs out on the grass, and compared their colours and the delicate patterns etched on them. Joel and Anne stood apart, talking in low voices, though Anne was only telling Joel of earlier egg-rollings. At length the rim of the sun appeared over the edge of the hill to their left, the oldest woman there gave the signal and they all launched their eggs down the hill, the children running beside theirs and encouraging them with shouts. Samuel tried to roll after his egg, but he was not of so convenient a shape, and kept turning sideways on and having to wriggle straight again. At last he sat up laughing.

'Sun dancing!' he said. The others looked at the sun, which was indeed clear of the horizon; but if it had danced Samuel was the only one who had seen it.

The egg-rollers sat down in groups, on cloaks spread on the dewy grass, and ate their eggs, well sprinkled with salt. It was lucky to get off as much of the shell whole as possible. Marion Barnard was jubilant, for her egg had rolled the furthest of all; but Martha's had hit a stone and turned aside.

The meal was taken in haste, for most of the party had to steal back to bed undiscovered. They ate, gathered up their cloaks and disappeared. Martha arranged to meet Marion, late on May Eve, to gather flowers in Wychwood, and make their May garlands together. Then they separated each to her party, and by the time the godly were abroad there was nothing to show of the egg-rolling except trampled grasses, with the crumbled egg-shells hidden among them.

The time to May Day went slowly for Martha, though it was not long. Mrs Widdison, filled with dreams of social success, was more determined than ever that her daughters should be accomplished young ladies, and Martha was held close to embroidery and dancing and music lessons. The household tasks, which she would have enjoyed, were, for the time at least, despised by her mother. Before May Day came Joel had good news from London. His father had been in correspondence with the Oxford authorities, and Joel was to be entered at Merton, and to go into residence as soon as possible. There was little time for him to prepare. Mrs Widdison was angry at the news, and obeyed the directions that her husband had sent as grudgingly as she dared. Joel would have been ill equipped if it had not been for Anne, who sat up late sewing every night for a week, and told him all she knew of the life at Oxford, and what he must expect there; though her information was but hearsay, and dated for the most part from before the War, — tales of her father's and cousins' college days. It seemed sad to her that he must go with so little cherishing, and with no family tradition behind him. Martha and Rachel would have worked for him heartily, if with little skill, but their mother held them close to their lessons, and was angry that there should be any bustle about Joel. Mr Widdison wrote that he would soon return, for they were assessing him for the full taxes as if his whole family were at home. The heavy taxation had driven many merchants from London, and in some ways it would be wiser to follow their example, but the unrest among the City Companies made it difficult to leave; the journeymen and yeomen were disaffected, and the Clothiers' Guild was as usual making claims against the Drapers, so that it was hard for a man to know what was best to do. In the meantime George Batchford was to look to the farm.

George Batchford grumbled at losing Joel's help on the farm as the busy time of the year was approaching, and Hobberdy Dick was but half pleased, though aware that Joel thought this a step to his permanent stay at Widford. He was to go on the 26th of April, a few days late for the beginning of term. On the night before he came into his room and found Anne and Charity packing his saddle bags with newly hemmed handkerchiefs and new shirts and cloth stockings.

'Thank you, Charity,' he said. 'And Mistress Seckar, I can never thank you enough for all you have done to set me on my way. I should have been in an ill plight if it hadn't been for you.'

'I wish we could have done better,' said Anne, 'but the time was short, and we had but the one roll of calico. You will know better what you need when you have been at Oxford a week or two; then if you write to George Batchford we will send it to you.'

Joel wanted to say more to her, but Charity was there, and when she slipped quietly from the room Anne went too. Joel followed her out into the passage.

'I shall be away early,' he said. 'So thank you again,

and good-bye. Think of me there, for it will be very new to me, and my Father says there are many temptations.'

'I will think of you,' said Anne.

Both were too shy to mention prayer, but it was prayer that they meant. They did not speak to each other again, but Anne watched him away next morning with a full heart, and Hobberdy Dick crouched above her on the gable end, watching too.

It was early sunny that day, and hot and clear all day, but it was a weather breeder. The next day the weather broke, and a week of cold rain began, very dashing to poor Martha's hopes. The night of May Eve was wetter than ever, and Rachel would not go with her, but Martha was of dogged stuff; at eleven o'clock she tiptoed downstairs, and slipped out of the pantry window as she had planned. Marion Barnard and a few others were in the Widford Wood, and they made for Widley's Copse, where they had agreed to meet some others, but it was a dismal excursion. The night was too dark for them to find flowers easily, and they stumbled through briars and into muddy ways. At length by common consent they left the copse, and made up through the thinner forest land towards Langley, to shelter under the ruins of the old Palace. In the darkness they wandered a little, and struck the road by Shipton Barrow.

'Keep right,' said Marion. 'The further from the gallows the better on May Eve.'

As she spoke a rush of wind and rain swept on them, and the children huddled together. Something shone palely from the tangled thicket of thorns that surrounded the old barrow. Above the rustle of the wind and the steady splash of the rain the children thought they heard a shrill, uncanny drone, and something dark passed close above them and into the thicket, as they crouched against the ground. Martha felt something tugging, softly but urgently, at her skirt, and, sturdy though she was, she knew that it was time to go home. She caught Marion's hand, and whispered low into her ear, 'Come on, tell the others and come.'

There was no need to communicate her fears; with a great scatter and trampling, like a herd of frightened calves, the children had fled, oversetting Marion as they went. Martha pulled her to her feet, and as she rose they saw a beam of pale light in which Mother Darke stood, close behind them.

'Never be afeard of me,' she said. 'Come, little maid, you'm a lucky face. Come, and us'll show you pretty things.'

Martha had no inclination to stay, and she pressed on, still plucked forward, and holding Marion by the hand; but Mother Darke seemed to hold her place without movement, and Martha walked with her head over her shoulder, and her eyes still held by Mother Darke's. Her left hand was stretched in front of her as she walked, and suddenly she felt it close on a twig. She swirled round and hit desperately at Mother Darke's face, which suddenly receded to far behind her, and disappeared. Martha and Marion broke into a run, slipping and squelching on the muddy track down towards Fulbrook. At Fulbrook they parted.

'I'll go in here,' said Marion, 'if so be you're not afeard to go on alone. 'Tis no night for Maying. Us were fools to try it.'

''Twill not be so bad for me going on,' said Martha, 'as 'twould be for you going back alone after seeing me in. Better luck next time.'

'You're proper brave and no mistake,' said Marion, and slipped in at her open window. Martha went on, still clutching the elder twig which had served her so well, and with a small hand still tugging steadily at her skirt. She climbed in at the window, and hid away the old clothes and shoes she had worn for the Maying, now sopping wet, until she could ask Charity to dry them. Then she crept shivering into bed, where she woke Rachel with her icy hands and feet. In the morning, however, her clothes were lying, dried and pressed, on the stool at the end of her bed, with her shoes, neatly cleaned, standing beneath it.

Fifteen

On three crosses of a tree
Three dead bodies hangèd be.
Two were thievis;
The third was Christ on whom we believis.
Dismas to Heaven went,
Gesmas to Hell was sent.
Christ it died on the Rood,
For Mary's love that by him stood;
And through the virtues of his blood
Jesus save us and our good;
Within and Without
And all place about,
And through the virtue of his might
Let no thief enter in this night.
No foot further than this ground
That I upon go,
But at my bidding there be found
To do all I bid them do.
Dark be their senses therewith,
And their lives mightless,
And their eyes sightless;
Dread and doubt
Then envelope about;
As a wall of stone
Be they cramped in the ton,
Cramp and crooking
And fault in their footing.
The might of the Trinity
Save these goods for me.

The Night Spell

MAY passed into June and Samuel Widdison still delayed his return. One thing after another arose to keep
him in Cheapside. So many of the Drapers' Company
were out of town that those left gained an influence

which he was loth to sacrifice. The time passed quietly at Widford. Mrs Widdison missed a man about the place, and as time went on would have been glad even of Joel. Whitsuntide came and went almost unnoticed. In the old days it had been a great time of rejoicing round Burford, too conspicuous to escape suppression. It was years now since the procession had formed to fetch the Whitsun buck from the forest lodge, and the great dragon had been burned in '41. Marion explained as much to Martha when she met her one June evening, gathering cowslips to make a face-cream for her mother.

'The next great day,' she said, 'is Midsummer Eve, when they sow hempseed, and those as has a mind go to the church door to see them pass as will die within the year.'

'That's a witch's trick,' said Martha. 'I wouldn't do that.'

'No more would I,' said Marion. 'I'd be afeard. They do say as how a party of them went to Taynton Church to watch one Midsummer Eve, and one on 'em fell asleep, nor nothing wouldn't wake her, and while she was asleep her likeness passed at the tail of the others. But she herself didn't know nothing, only a kind of deadness had comed over her. But her died two days afore the year was out. No, 'tis ill meddling with the dead; but I'd dearly love to set a meal of beer and cheese for my true love to come and eat.'

'My granny did use to say,' said Martha, 'that the future is in God's hand, and we had no call to know more.'

''Tis gospel truth,' said Marion. 'But there's one thing us can do on Midsummer Eve that has no harm to it, we could go to see the great bonfire the gipsies raise at midnight. My dad does say as how 'tis the worship of Baal; but there's no harm in watching when we don't bring so much as a twig. 'Tis a rare sight, so 'tis, if so be you're not afeard.'

'I'm none afeard,' said Martha. 'But I'll not bring Samuel for fear the gipsies should steal him away. I'll slip out after we're bedded, and meet you on the way to Widley Copse.'

On Midsummer Eve George Batchford was busy, and Hobberdy Dick with him, protecting the stock and farmsteading against witches, and the ill-will of the dead. Bored flints were hung over the mangers, except over that where Dick usually sat, and fresh elder twigs, gathered with permission asked of the tree, were stuck into the horseshoes over the doors. Nor did George Batchford on this night omit the night spell, spoken to protect land and stock against witchcraft or theft.

> 'On three crosses of a tree
>   Three bodies hanging be,'

he muttered, and so through to the end.

Dick, pleased to see all so well performed, went back late to the house to see if Anne was safely asleep. For once he did not go to see the children in their beds, for he was tired with seeking for self-bored flints, and setting them where George could find them. He curled himself in a corner by Anne's bed, and fell asleep. He was awakened suddenly about midnight by the sound of his name, and the feeling that he was being drawn swiftly away. Before him he saw a light that illuminated nothing, and far off, though with increasing volume, he heard a voice saying, 'I, Malkin Ferrisher, called Mother Darke, do adjure thee, Hobberdy Dick, by Sathanell, Azazell and Balzebub, and by the most dreadful Rhadamanthus, Prince of Hell....' Dick's feet were being swept from under him. He snatched desperately at Anne's bed to stop himself, caught at her hair, and then her hand. The voice diminished in volume, though he could still hear faintly, 'do appear in this crystal glass, meekly and mildly, to do all things that I may demand of you. . . .' Anne woke alarmed, and cried, 'Our Lord bless and preserve us!' She felt a small, thin hand clutching hers convulsively, but though the pale moonlight lit her room she could see nothing. The witch light died away from before Dick's eyes, the moonlight again illuminated the room, and the strange voice was silent. Still he dared not loose Anne's hand. It was no wonder that Anne was frightened, to feel that clinging which she could not see, but there was an urgency in the clutch which forbade her to snatch her hand away. She steadied her voice, and said gently, 'God bless you, whoever you may be.' The grasp relaxed, and Dick crouched down by her bed, relieved from compulsion, but unwilling to go far from her protection. As his panic subsided the power of reflection returned. How had this voice broken through the protection of the night spell unless someone belonging to the house was outside, and his departure had broken a way though the barrier? If so, whoever it was, willingly or unwillingly, must be in contact with Mother Darke. It was his duty to go and see, yet he hardly dared to leave the protection of Anne's blessing. It would do no good to anyone if he were to be imprisoned within Mother Darke's crystal stone, to do her ugly bidding for ever.

He caught Anne's hand, swarmed up onto the bed, and whispered urgently into her ear: 'Do 'ee come and look.' The voice was so low that Anne thought it was only inside her head. For all that she obeyed it, confident in the friendliness of the presence in the room. She got up, put her feet into slippers, drew her cloak about her and opened her door. Something tugged at her cloak, and drew her to look at the maids, and then into old Ursula's room. All quiet and safe there, all asleep. Then they went downstairs and into the children's room. The nurse was sound asleep, with the baby curled up in his crib beside her – he was beginning to outgrow it. In the little girls' bed Diligence was asleep close against the wall, and Rachel at the outer edge; but the central place, which should have held Martha, was cold and empty. Dick smote his breast. He had known Mother Darke had an eye to Martha: what had possessed him not to guard her on Walpurgis night, when all the powers of witchcraft were abroad? Martha, the flower of the flock! He pictured her dazed and entranced, captured to act as scryer to the crystal which should have held him. He loosed hold of Anne – this was no time to think of his own safety – and shot downstairs, as quick as summer lightning. Anne followed him more slowly, and found the open pantry window by which Martha had gone out.

In the meantime Hobberdy Dick was down at the stable, throwing stones against the loft window. 'Batchford! George Batchford! Thee's wanted below!' he cried again and again in his piping tones. At length he heard a stir within, and before long George Batchford thrust out his head.

'Who's that below?' he said, but Hobberdy Dick was gone. He had snatched up an unused sprig of elder, and was off towards Taynton. The Taynton Lob would help him, and maybe old Grim of Stow could advise them out of his stores of experience. The humans must manage the affair in their own way, but he would rouse all the hobs in the countryside if need be to get Martha Widdison out of the hands of the witches.

In the meantime George Batchford had pulled on his clothes, and brought an unlit lantern into the house, to kindle it at the kitchen fire. He found Anne there.

'Was it you as called me, mistress?' he said.

'No,' said Anne, 'but I need you. Little Martha is not in her bed.'

'Tush, make naught of that,' he said. ''Tis Midsummer Eve, and likely her will have gone off with the Fulbrook children, to gather fernseed of the fairies, or such like children's gear.'

'Yes, I should have thought so,' said Anne, 'but I was strangely and urgently wakened, and it seems to me that something must be amiss.'

'I said the night spell tonight,' said George Batchford. 'I doubt me her'll not get back through it before sunrise. Likely she's held cramped somewhere. The poor little maid would be sore frittened.'

'It's best not to use spells, good or bad,' said Anne. 'Prayers are enough. We had best go out and look for her. If we can find her before she is missed we shall save her punishment.'

'Take a crust of bread with you,' said George Batchford. ''Tis an ill night to be afield. I wish we had some holy water, but there's none to be had in the church these days. Milk is the next best, and I'll take a can.'

'A good thought!' said Anne. 'If the child is tired and spent it may serve us well too. Do you get them while I run up and dress.'

They went round the boundary fields together, but no one was held there with cramp and crooking and fault in their footing. It took them some time to go round, and by the time they had finished the moon had set.

'Where would it be best to seek? There are ferns in

Widley Copse, if she has gone to gather fernseed. The chief place for the fairies is the Rollright Stones, but she could never go so far.'

'She'd none be such a fool as to go to Gallowshill on Midsummer Eve,' said George Batchford, 'and Worsley Bottom is pretty near as bad. Or they may have gone to Aston Barrow. 'Tis to look for a needle in a haystack and no mistake.'

'Well, let's go up to Widley Copse first of all,' said Anne, 'and if we can find no one there we'll turn back, and see if she has got home without us.'

The night was fine and still, and they searched and called through Widley Copse, rousing an owl to answer them, but with no other success, and in the increasing anxiety which a fruitless search arouses. Then they turned back and searched the nearer woods, and after looking into the house and finding that Martha was not yet home, they went down to the river, and into the little copse where Mr Widdison had been led astray at Christmas time.

'What's our Dick been doing?' said George Batchford bitterly. 'I'd a sworn he had a kindly eye on the child.'

'I think it was he that wakened me,' said Anne.

'Come to think of it, I do believe he called me too. 'Tis urgent. There's second cock-crow. In an hour's time or two she's bound to be back if naught has gone amiss.'

'We'll wait till two hours after sunrise,' said Anne, 'and if she's not back then I'll go down to the Barnard child at Fulbrook, she will be at work by then, – and see if Martha was with them last night; and do you send Ned to Oxford to fetch the young master home. If she is not back by seven o'clock we can no longer keep it secret from her mother.'

They went into the house, and prepared food, and ate a little. While they were still waiting Charity came down to blow up the fire, and found it lit. She knew no more of Martha's plans than the other two, and at half past five Anne set out for Fulbrook, to find Marion Barnard as quietly as possible, and learn whether she had been with Martha. George Batchford met her on her return at the top of the fields.

'Any news?' he said. 'Ned's ready to go, but I waited to send him off till such time as you were back.'

'They went together to see the gipsies' bonfire in Wychwood,' said Anne. 'Marion Barnard says they walked into a thick mist on the way home, and when she got to the edge of it she heard Martha say she would go home alone, and they parted. She was loth to tell anything for fear of her father; but I drew her aside, and got that much out of her.'

'There was no natural mist last night,' said George Batchford. 'Her should have known better, native bred as her be.'

'I think she was frightened, and ready to believe that Martha could make her own way home,' said Anne. 'I must go and tell her mother.'

When she got home, however, she found the bad news before her. The nursemaid had wakened and missed Martha; there had been an uproar among the servants, and Rachel had told something of what she knew. Mrs Widdison was already dressed as far as her morning gown, and was sending out the servants to search in strong distress. Anne's news, such as it was, could bring little comfort. Ned was dispatched to Oxford, Jonathon Fletcher went, at Anne's suggestion, to Burford, to rouse the constable and George Batchford went towards Wychwood, meaning to gather help on his way, to search the gipsies' camp, in case Martha had been carried off. On Anne's suggestion, too, Mrs Widdison sent a note across to Lady Fettiplace, begging her to set some of her men about the search. But it seemed, as George Batchford had said, to be hunting a needle in a bundle of hay.

Sixteen

When candles burne both blue and dim,
Old folkes will say, Here's fairy Grim.

The Life of Robin Goodfellow

HOBBERDY DICK had no difficulty in finding the
Taynton Lob, who was couched snug in his own
church tower. The difficulty was to persuade him to
stir abroad on Midsummer Eve, and on so perilous an
errand. He reminded Dick how they had been put to
flight a year ago last May Day, and that witchcraft was
much stronger at this season; but the Lob was good-
natured, and Dick, strengthened by a human blessing,
overbore his objections. He gave Lob a leaf from his
elder twig, and they set out together. There was no one
of much consequence at Barrington, so they made
straight up the hill towards Stow. At Iccomb they
turned aside to pick up Patch of Iccomb, who had a
fairy horn with which he could summon such other
hobs as might be stirring abroad. He was a brisk fellow, and glad of the prospect of a bicker. The moon
had set, however, before they reached Stow churchyard, and found old Grim, playing a subdued and
melancholy air upon the bones.

It took a long time to explain the matter to him;
Patch's horn had summoned some half-dozen spirits
before Dick and Lob succeeded in convincing him that
Martha had been carried off not by the fairies but by
witches. When he fully understood them his partisan-
ship was aroused. This was no mere matter between
humans, for whom Grim cared little enough by this

time, but an attempt against the realm of fairy, in which Hobberdy Dick himself had nearly been carried away.

'A murrion on them!' he cried. 'And may the lightning blast their circle and the fire freeze aneath their cauldron! What right have they to meddle with the likes of we?'

He drew himself up to a greater height than they had ever seen him, and green fire flashed from his eye-sockets. His companions shrank back from him with something like amazement. They began to recollect the days when Grim's Ditch had stretched from the forest to Alvescot, and he had been a god rather than a hob.

'What shall us do, Grim?' said Hobberdy Dick, with even greater respect than usual.

'Second cock-crow be at hand,' said Grim. 'All those that be bound by it leap home to bed; those that be free scour round the barrows that have lost their spirits. There's more that use the hollow hills than the like of we. And meet me at Rollright tomorrow night when the moon casts the shadow of the stones.'

He shook himself, and a shaggy, black dog, as large as a calf and with fiery eyes, stood for a moment in his place, and then sprang over the churchyard wall and was gone. Four of the spirits vanished in obedience to his command, the remaining five drew into the shelter of Grim's tomb and consulted together.

''Twas at Shipton Barrow that Mother Darke did set eye on her last,' said Dick. 'That be a favourite place for the witches, for 'tis by Habber Gallows Hill; but they do shift their ground here and there. Then there's the Long Barrow near Leafield; will 'ee look there, Lull, 'tis not far from Kingstanding; and there's the old work beyond Cornbury, where Drip did use to bide afore he was laid; would 'ee look there too.'

'And I'll do Maugerbury Camp and Cornhill,' said Patch; 'and there's Knollbury Camp and Lyneham; Hairy Tib of Bruern can do them both; and have a look-see at the Hawkstone, Tib, while you'm about it.'

''Tis not likely they'll cross the Windrush,' said Dick, 'but I'll go to the Asthall Mound, and the Great Camp at Windrush.'

'And I'll go to Eastington Barrow and Norbury,' said another Lob, 'and see if I can pick up any news at Woeful Lake. There's a nixie there do know more than most.'

'I'll go to Shipton Barrow,' said the Taynton Lob bravely. 'It seems to me 'tis there they're most like to be; and they haven't got a hold of my name like they have of Dick's.'

'No, Lob, thee's a cunning one,' said Tib of Bruern, 'and have holden on to thy name so long that even the rest of we can hardly call it to mind.'

Lob grinned at this compliment, and they parted on their various ways, moving furtively, and taking cover under elder trees whenever they could find them. Luckily the hedges had been little trimmed since the wars, and the hobs had seen to it that the elders sprang up apace.

It was full day by the time that Hobberdy Dick got to Widford, where he paused for a short time to look in before crossing the river to Asthall Mound. The household was all in confusion, and none of the men to be seen; but George Batchford had looked to the stock before setting out. Dick fed the hens, whom Charity had forgotten, and then went downstream to cross the river by Swinbrook bridge. It was difficult to be sure by daylight, the ghosts were all at rest and there was no one to give information, but he could find no trace of the witches' visitation there, nor at Windrush. He crossed the Windrush at Barrington, and looked in to Taynton churchyard to see if the Lob was at home. He was still away, however, and Dick went up to the Shipton Barrow, and met him there.

'They've been here within two-three nights,' he said, 'and in the old quarry yonder; but there's no saying if they were here last night, and there's no entering the mound till moonlight. Us must try it tonight.'

'Till tonight, then,' said Dick, and they parted.

Dick went pondering home. Suppose that Martha was spell-bound within the barrow there, it would be no easy matter to free her. It was no hard thing to free a mortal from fairy-land, for mortals had so many weapons. There was cold iron, and holy water, and bread and spittle and salt. Some of these the witches feared a little, but their mortal blood stood them in good stead, and they had a dozen ways of evading these counter-charms. Many times they stood firm even against Holy Writ, for they had their own ways of twisting it to ill. Besides, which of the hobs could use these human spells? And for the fairy weapons, the traitorous bogles who served the witches, and the poor spirits whom they had enslaved, could wield these with the best of them. To enlist mortal help would be best, and that would not be easy to do. If only the old lady were alive, he thought, she would know what was best to be done.

So poor Joel thought, whom Dick found already arrived when he returned. He was trying at once to devise a plan of action and to comfort and encourage his stepmother, who was entreating and scolding by turns, and crying all the while. She would hardly give him time to consult with Anne and George Batchford, and find out what was best to do, and what had been done. At length he persuaded her to lie down and rest a little in Anne's care, for she was really ill and fevered with crying, while he went to fetch Marion Barnard. He explained to her father that she and Martha had sometimes gone about together, and gave him a shilling to allow her to come and show him the places where they had gone. He brought her back, pale and tongue-tied, and he and George Batchford went with her over the way which they had taken the night before. She was not quite sure where they had run into mist, but it was not far from Shipton Barrow. She changed colour when she saw how near it was, and said urgently, 'Come away, come within doors, and I'll tell 'ee summat.'

She would say no more until she had taken them right back to Widford; and in the stable there, well guarded by its horseshoes, she at length broke silence.

''Twas up by that very barrow as Mother Darke comed after us on May Eve, wheedling and coaxing of us to come back with her. And she did come on close beside us till Martha struck her face with an elder twig, and she did vanish clean away, and us did run home so fast as we could run. And I can tell you no more, but I know she had a mind to Martha.' She burst out crying as she spoke, and sobbed bitterly, 'But Martha was too true-hearted to go along with the likes of she.'

'We know she was,' said Joel. 'Do you know anything of this old woman, George?'

'Mother Darke be the wickedest old hag in Wychwood,' said George Batchford, 'and that's saying a deal. No man don't know where she bides, or I'd a fetched a wisp of her thatch and burned it right now. 'Tis a sure way to bring a witch if she have ill-willed you.'

''Tis best not to meet spells with spells,' said Joel.

'There must be some right way of freeing her. Don't cry, Marion. What you have told us may be a good help to us. Run to Charity in the kitchen, and she will give you a piece of cake and a drink of milk before you go home.'

When she had gone, still sobbing, across the yard George Batchford and Joel looked questioningly at each other. George Batchford's face was pale and grim, and he had a bandage over one eye, for the gipsies had actively resented the search of their camp.

'Do you think it can be so, George?' said Joel. 'What could the witches want with a good child like Martha, and would they be so mad as to rouse Justice against them? Why a few years back the very name of a witch was fatal to anyone.'

'Aye, in most places,' said George Batchford. 'But there's old, old things there, and more hiding places than the keepers know of. As for what use they'd make of her, they witches has darker purposes than the likes of we can guess. Maybe they're after the Widford treasure, there was a sight of it hidden here in the old days they say. But never fear, Master, we'll get her back, and before we're much older. There's those about are good friends to us, and while the young mistress is in the house naught can go far amiss.'

'In the meantime,' said Joel, 'we will search the Barrow again, and the quarries behind it.'

'Best wait till moonrise,' said George Batchford, 'and go carefully. Us don't want to frighten them away. I'll attend to the stock.'

Marion's news gave more satisfaction to Hobberdy Dick than to the others, for it confirmed Lob's findings. It was now nearly certain that Martha had been caught near the Barrow, and in all probability she was still beneath it. The Barrow was one of the hollow places that had long lost its proper occupant; and when a gentle spirit deserts a place an evil one is almost certain to possess it. Joel and George Batchford were to go there at night, and George could be trusted to take salt and a horseshoe and elder branches. He wondered if he would bring a Bible, and if he knew what verses to read. If he did Dick thought that between them they could free Martha. But he was not sure of the verses, nor did he know how he could convey them, unless one of these humans would settle down and go to sleep, and that they showed no signs of doing, except Mrs Widdison, whose mind was impermeable, awake or asleep. Dick was wiser than the mortals. He knew that he had done all that he could do until he had held counsel with old Grim, and that he would need all his strength and energy that night. He curled himself up on a beam of the well-guarded stable and went to sleep.

Seventeen

Mongst graves and grottes, neare an old charnell house,
Where you shall find her sitting in her forme,
As fearfull and melancholique as that
She is about; with Caterpillers kells,
And knottie cobwebs, rounded in with spells.

BEN JONSON, *The Sad Shepherd*

As soon as the moon was strong enough to cast a dark
shadow of the Rollright Stones on the grass the lobs
met in conclave. Dick and Lob of Taynton came first,
with Patch of Iccomb, who joined them as they climbed
the hill. All were assembled, with the exception of one
small, night-haunting hob who was not to be seen,
when a dark, gaunt form came loping over the grass,
and Grim, assuming his proper shape, crouched in the
shadow of the tallest stone. The hobs gave their reports
in turn. What evidence there was corroborated Dick's
and the Taynton Lob's. Witches had passed from every
point in a direction centring on the Shipton Barrow,
though there was no direct evidence that their meeting
had been at Gallows Hill.

'But Gallows Hill or no,' said Dick, 'Shipton Barrow's the hollow place nearest to it. If they be gone
underground 'tis likely 'tis there they'll be. But how
to get at 'em is another story; and 'tis there we look to
thee, Grim.'

'Give I a drink of may dew,' said old Grim, 'and then
grip hands in a circle; for I have a power of work behind me, and 'tis a clear head I need, and all the
strength your hands can give to say my tale aright.'

They dispersed, and returned in a minute with

hands abrim with may dew, which each offered in turn to old Grim. Then they crouched in a circle, hand locked in hand, and swayed slightly. Old Grim, with his eyes closed, swayed with them, then stopped rigid and opened his eyes, from which a green light now blazed.

'I've been about and about,' he said, 'this way and that; and I've learned all there is to know about Mother Darke. She'm a learned witch, the head of all the witches in these parts, but she've pretty well reached the end of her tether. She'm a two-ways witch, and such is always in more peril, for their devils loathe 'em. She've sold her soul right enough, and has her things what suck her, same as any old black witch as you might name. But her's not content with that, for her's as proud as one we'll not mention. So her's dug her circles and carved her sigils, and bound her spirits to her, good and bad. And her's so testy and tetchy, they must skip this way and that with never a civil word, till they hate her very shoestrings, one and all. But she've over-reached herself, so she have, when she tried to bind an honest hob to her service. She knows right well how they hate her, and except for one or two impets that she suckles, there's not a one she dare treat with without she stands in her circle with her rod in her hand. And that, I take it, is how she've looked round for a milder spirit to treat with, and how she tried to catch our Dick. Tonight, I take it, in the full of the moon, the hill will be open, and she'll be trying her spells, with the mortal child as scryer. 'Twill be easy for us to get into the hill, Dick, and if so be as you can get quietly close to the circle, I'll terrify her so her'll start a little back, and do 'ee snatch her rod so soon as it comes clear of the circle, and then her'll have no more power on 'ee never more.'

'But what about Martha?' said Dick. ' 'Tis her we're seeking to free.'

'I don't know naught about her,' said Grim. 'If so be you have the rod, 'tis likely you can free her, but I knows naught.'

'I've heard tell,' said Patch, 'that human must free human, and it must be by book. They say there is a piece that will do it; but I don't know which. Maybe mortals could tell.'

'There's no time to be lost,' said Dick. 'I must go get mortal help from Widford. Could 'ee give us a back, Grim,' he said pleadingly. 'I'd not ask it, but mortals move so fearful slow, and they must be up there afore the moon sets.'

'Maybe,' said the Taynton Lob, 'the old witch's imps will tell on thee, Dick, as thee comes up to the circle, and then 'twill go hard. Maybe 'tis the very trap she've set.'

'I can't help for that,' said Dick. 'It must be tried, whether or no.'

'Hold out thy hand, Dick,' said a voice, close at his ear. Dick held out his hands, something fell tickling into the palms, and the Shining Boy of Widley Copse appeared to the company. At the same moment Dick disappeared, as the precious fernseed touched his hands. The hobs laughed and cheered, and crowded round the Shining Boy with congratulations. Grim shook himself and leapt to his feet, Dick scrambled on to his shaggy back with some difficulty, keeping his fists still clenched, and the great creature bounded towards Widford.

By the time they reached it Joel, George Batchford and Jonathon Fletcher had set out for the Barrow, George loaded with every countercharm which occurred to him. The women servants were in the kitchen, Rachel and Diligence crouched down with them by the fire. Martha's bed was ready for her, with hot bricks in it, and a skillet was standing by the fire. No one was asleep there, for old Ursula was fidgeting to and fro, sending the servants on this errand or that, though there was nothing left to do. Even little Diligence, who had as a rule a great talent for sleep, was kept awake by her bustle. Neither Anne nor Mrs Widdison was in the room, and Dick went upstairs to look for them. Here at length fortune was propitious. Anne had longed with all her heart to go up to the Barrow with the men to look for Martha, but Mrs Widdison could not be left. Grief and suspense had made her really ill, and her tears could only be stayed by constant attention. Anne had succeeded at length in getting her to take some spoonfuls of milk and wine, and had read her to sleep. Now she was sitting with the Bible before her; but the enforced stillness, her wakeful night and busy, anxious day, had overpowered her senses, and she was dozing.

She had sat there only a minute, with her head bowed over her book, when she heard a voice say loud and clear beside her, 'Search the Scriptures! Go up and read it at the old Barrow! Make haste! Make haste!'

She started, wide awake in a moment, or so it seemed to her, and rose to her feet without haste or delay. She had no doubt of the passage; the Bible was open at Luke 10, and in verses 17 to 20 she saw what would help her if anything could. She carried it with her, still open, and set off running, up the field track to the copse, straight across the Swinbrook road, and through the fields to Fulbrook Gap, and thence up the road to the Barrow. Dick did not wait for her. As soon as he saw that his message was delivered he ran back to Grim, and scrambled again upon his back. The moonlit fields flashed past them, and they were soon at the thorny thicket which hid the Barrow. It was a busy scene, to their eyes at least. The mortals were there, searching the small scrub of twisted thorns, and the friendly hobs were already in their places, hidden here and there where a propitious plant afforded shelter, and ready to give what help they could. The mortals saw neither them nor the pillars upon which the Barrow was raised, for strong blinding spells hid these from honest human eyes. Dick slid off the black dog's back, and Grim resumed his usual form. He held out his hand, and Dick opened his right hand into it. Invisible to mortal and fairy eyes alike, they went into the hill.

Shipton Barrow was small, but it gave entrance to a much wider space; and they saw a great but dark cave, without the gaieties of fairy habitation, lit only by corpse-lights and touchwood. This night Mother Darke was without colleagues, it may be that she pursued secrets too potent, or wealth too great, to be shared. But though she worked alone the cave was busy. Dick at the first glance had seen Martha crouched on the ground and staring entranced into a crystal of moon-stone. A raven was perched on a projecting tree-root, and two small green creatures in a basket of wool cocked their ears and watched. These were her famil-iars, and were chiefly to be feared by the hobs. Mother Darke was in a terrene circle, with her rod in her hand and surrounded by a diverse crowd of imps, those whom she addressed crouching before her, and those behind her clawing vainly at the circle. At her feet was the bath of blood, and terrible words streamed from her lips. A smaller circle had been made on the ground before her, and into this it was evident that something was to be conjured. Dick stole up to the

circle behind the witch, as near as he could to the noxious spirits, and fixed his eyes upon the wand. He could no longer see Grim, but guessed where he would go. The conjuration continued. Suddenly, between the two circles and near to the witch, a monstrous shape appeared, with flaming jaws and eyes, larger than a panther and rampant, so that his great paw came higher than her head. It was utterly unexpected, and the witch faltered backward. Dick snatched for her wand, but her demons had been quicker. A claw caught her skirt and another her heel; there were unearthly yells and gibberings and squeaks, a sudden swirling chaos was opened beneath them, Dick leapt back just in time; the lights went out, and all was darkness and silence, except for the flapping and dismal cries of the raven, and small squeals from the green creatures. The hobs ran in from outside with a faint light of glow-worms, and found old Grim stretched upon the floor, exhausted by this final effort. But Martha knelt on by her crystal stone, and the wand which might have freed her was gone.

Eighteen

What have ye let the false enchanter scape?
O ye mistook, ye should have snatcht his wand
And bound him fast; without his rod revers't,
And backward mutters of dissevering power,
We cannot free the Lady that sits here
In stony fetters fixt, and motionless.

JOHN MILTON, *Comus*

JOEL and George Batchford had set off for the Barrow
shortly after sundown, followed, rather under protest,
by Jonathon Fletcher, who saw no sense in this lurking
about draughty hillsides. They reached the Barrow at
about ten, when the first stars were showing, and the
strengthening moon had begun to cast a shadow. They
searched the place again, treading cautiously and
speaking in whispers; then they set Jonathon to watch
behind the nearest hedgerow, under the shelter of a
wild plum tree, and went on to search the quarries,
both the old, disused ones near at hand and the newer
quarries that were still being worked. Then they
climbed to Habber Gallows Hill, where the bones of
Ned Lightfoot of Leafield were still dangling, clear in
the moonshine, to see if there was any fold or thicket
which could conceal a witch's hovel. As they returned
from this fruitless quest Jonathon came running across
the open space to meet them.

'I saw something,' he said, much shaken. 'Something
went past me into the thicket, and I heard as it might
be a kind of laugh.'

'Quick, where did it go?' said Joel.

'Into the thicket there, round the old mound; but

I wouldn't venture there, not for a hundred pounds, and no more shouldn't you, master.'

'There's more at stake here nor a hundred pound,' said George Batchford sternly; but Jonathon still hung back. George tossed him a crust of bread for a guard, and he and Joel plunged again into the thicket, as quietly as might be. They searched the place to and fro, inch by inch, for what seemed hours, but there was no sign of human footing, though sometimes there were strange rustlings beside them, hard to account for in the stillness of that night. George noticed some stinkpot toadstools, and, tracing them round, found that they encircled the barrow. He began to sprinkle salt on them, one by one; but it was a slow business, for they were hard to find in the uncertain moonshine and thick undergrowth. Before he was half round them they heard a sound like a landslide in the quarry, with a more sinister echo like the shriek of a storm. They came together, heedless for the moment of the noise they made.

'Was it in the quarry, do you think?' said Joel.

'Nay,' said George. 'It sounded to me more like under our feet. God guard the little maiden.'

There was a rush past them, a little dancing of faint light, and as they strained their ears they thought they heard a confusion of faint sounds, high pitched and almost inaudible like the cries of bats.

'She's here! She's here!' cried Joel in despair. 'And we can't get through to her. What can we do, George?'

'Sprinkle salt and pray, master,' said George. ''Tis the likeliest thing to avail now.'

They stood together, each murmuring his prayers, though George Batchford's were mostly an adaptation of the White Paternoster. Their devotions were broken by the sound of a girl's voice speaking breathlessly in the direction where they had left Jonathon Fletcher. The hope came to them that it was Martha, and they both ran towards it; but it was Anne Seckar, breathless and muddied, with an open Bible in her hand. She thrust it into Joel's, gasping, 'Read, read from there; I have no breath.'

The moonlight was not bright enough for him to read by it, and they spent some time lighting their lantern, while Anne lay panting on the·turf. At length the light was strong enough, and Joel read. 'Again,' said Anne when he reached the end of the passage. He read it again, and began a third time; but he had not reached the end before a faint light appeared from the barrow in front of them, and Martha came walking steadily towards them, with her eyes open and her hands outstretched. Joel snatched her up in his arms and threw his cloak about her, and she seemed to come to herself.

Two solicitous processions set out from the Barrow that night in opposite directions, one carrying Martha and one old Grim of Stow. Dick was torn between them, but in the end his gratitude conquered, and he went with the hobs. They bore old Grim to his favourite tomb, washed him from head to foot with may dew, rubbed him down with wild thyme, and, as he revived, gave him as much dew to drink as he could quaff. Gradually his shrivelled form expanded, and he looked around him with a livelier air. Indeed old Grim was the brisker, the stronger and the more alert for that night's work for a hundred years to come.

In the meantime George Batchford and Joel carried Martha home by turns. She was still dazed and silent. Jonathon Fletcher hurried on ahead to tell the good news. The household came out in a clamour of relief and curiosity, and Mrs Widdison, running downstairs in her stuff gown, caught Martha in her arms and kissed her repeatedly, exclaiming; 'You naughty, naughty child! Where have you been? You deserve to be well whipped. I have been nearly dead with anxiety for you, and it is unknown what your father will say. Where have you been?'

'She is not fully herself, madam,' said Anne Seckar. 'We had better give her some warm milk and put her to bed, had we not? We will tell you about it when she is asleep.'

Martha drank the warmed milk that was waiting for her, and as she gave back the cup looked at Anne and said; 'Where is the deep pool that I was looking in? Didn't I ought to be back there? I was waiting for someone.'

But she hardly waited for Anne's reassurance before she fell asleep.

It was no easy matter to explain to Mrs Widdison what had happened, the more so as none of them quite knew what it was. It was however pretty clear that Mother Darke had had some share in the business, and Mrs Widdison wrote frantically to her husband to come home and take over the prosecution. George Batchford was unwilling to bring the matter to trial. He admitted that it was common knowledge that a witch lost her power as soon as the Law took her in hand, but Mother Darke was not the only witch in the countryside, and he had no desire to fall foul of them. The machinery however had already been set in motion, and though the constables did not care to penetrate too far into Wychwood, they found what they thought to be Mother Darke's hovel, and collected a few wax images and sigils in the straw of the bed; but they did not find the witch herself. By the time Samuel Widdison came home the pursuit was beginning to die down, and though he stirred it for a while into activity no trace of Mother Darke was found; nor was she ever seen in those parts again.

Nineteen

Some say the fairies fair
Did dance on Bednall Green,
And fine familiars of the air
Did talk with men unseen.

THOMAS CHURCHYARD

IN spite of having been called away from the thick of
his work and of the uncanny business on which he had
been summoned Samuel Widdison returned in a complacent humour. By the time he arrived Martha was
almost recovered from the strange lassitude that had
hung over her for a few days after her rescue. Her
mother scolded and petted her alternately, but Samuel
Widdison, after a talk with Joel, commanded that no
more be said on the subject, and merely told Martha
that there must be no more running abroad, and that
she must be thankful to have escaped so slightly. Joel
and Anne were relieved that she had escaped both
punishment and further question, for they felt that
she was delicately poised upon the edge of much
mental suffering, and that very little would precipitate
her into it.

'I am so thankful,' said Anne, 'that Mother Darke
has not been found, for I dread that Martha should be
questioned as a witness. I think she knows nothing of
what happened to her, and it would be a terrible thing
for her to learn.'

Joel shuddered.

'Yes, indeed,' he said. 'God keep any child from
being dragged into a witch trial. From what I hear the

prickers and questioners and witch-hunters are pretty near as bad as the witches. I wouldn't have poor little Martha in such company to save her life.'

The reason of Mr Widdison's complacent mood was soon made clear to Joel, and, as it happened, to Hobberdy Dick. Joel and his father had returned from Burford market, where they had bought a few sheep which George Batchford was to drive home. As Joel rubbed down the horses with newly acquired skill his father said to him:

'I am well pleased with the way in which the farm prospers, boy. It seems to me you have learned something of management, and I understand you are doing not amiss at Oxford either, and am glad that you have no debts to confess to me. It seems that you are beginning to show to a man; and since business has been prospering well I have it in mind to look around for a wife for you.'

'A wife, sir,' faltered Joel. 'Sure I have no need of a wife while I am still a colleger.'

'No hurry about the marriage itself,' said his father, 'but no harm to have the thing arranged. What do you say to Alderman Peto's Joan? A pretty enough girl, well taught and of a godly household, and but two years older than yourself. Her father is ready enough for the match, and it would be an advantage to you in many ways. Your consequence would be much increased, both here and in London, and the dowry, with what I would put to it, would secure you an immediate income.'

'Indeed, sir, indeed, Father,' said Joel in much agitation, 'I thank you for your kindness. I know it is all meant in care for me; but I have no mind to Joan Peto; I could not bring myself to think of marrying her.'

'And why not, pray?' said his father sternly. 'What fault have you to find in the wife chosen for you by your father? Have you let your fancy stray about the countryside? Or been making love to some innkeeper's daughter in Oxford. If so it is time indeed that you were settled.'

'No, no, it is no such matter,' said Joel. 'But I pray you, sir, set it aside for a little. Indeed I am too young to marry yet.'

'Time will mend that,' said his father. 'That is fool's talk. Where his fortune serves him a man is best to wed betimes; then he and his wife grow together. I have broached the matter already to the Alderman, and he is well pleased with the notion. It cannot be set aside for any such silly, idle reasons.'

'Joan Peto is fat and dark and red-faced,' said Joel wildly. 'She is city-bred, and would never be happy in the country. We should be wretched if we married.'

'I will not hear you further tonight,' said his father. 'I have always thought you a good, dutiful boy, and when you have recollected yourself I doubt not I shall find you so still. Say no more of it now, and tomorrow or next day we will speak of it again. If you spoke the truth when you assured me that you had no other love you will have doubtless thought better of it then. Say no more now, and assure yourself that it is for your good and your advancement.'

He left the stable as he spoke, and Joel seated himself on a saddleblock with his head in his hands. Hobberdy Dick slipped out of the shadows and stole to his side. And both knew at the same moment why it was that no dark, round-faced girl might come to be mistress at Widford.

The illumination brought little comfort to Joel, but merely set him another problem to solve. He knew that

155

he loved Anne Seckar, and was sure that there was no other wife anywhere in the world for him, and that, missing her, he must die a bachelor; but how to move in the matter was another thing. It was more than two years before he would be of age. Even if she returned his love he would be unable to marry her or protect her before then; and if, as was more probable, she had no liking for him any offer of affection would be both an insult and an injury. It was impossible that he should marry Joan Peto; and yet for a son to refuse the arrangement made for him by an affectionate and careful father was the height of undutifulness. He sat for an hour on the block in the stable almost without moving, with Dick at his side; and at the end was no nearer to a solution than ever. All he could determine was to play for time.

The next few days were disagreeable for both Joel and his father. The greater stress was Joel's, but Mr Widdison hated to be at odds with his son, and was disappointed that his affectionate designs were so ungratefully received. It was vacation time, so that there was nothing to call Joel back to Oxford, and Mr Widdison renewed the attack again and again, unwilling to return to London until he could make definite proposals to Alderman Peto. Joel on his side only begged his father to settle nothing until he was older. He pointed out that he wished for nothing except time, but he begged for that with an urgency that made his father suspicious. Dick racked his brains, but could think of no immediate way of helping him; Samuel Widdison had always been of obdurate stuff. Joel was not without an ally, however, though she was an unexpected one. His stepmother opposed the match with all her heart. She had no wish to increase Joel's consequence, and she hated the notion of a daughter-in-law in the house, and of Joan Peto above all, who was a bustling, capable girl, good-humoured enough, but with a high notion of her own importance. Between the two Mr Widdison was defeated, for the time at least; and, after four days of argument and counter-argument, he set out for London, with a half promise that he would let the matter lapse for the present; and Joel was free to attend to the sheep-shearing. He had the time for which he had asked, and that should have satisfied him; but he found that it did not. Now that he knew how it was with him he was perpetually hungry for the sight of Anne, and longed always to be talking with her. He felt that if he could only know for certain that she counted herself his friend it would be enough for him, and he would not aspire to her love. At the same time he knew that this would not be enough, that, once satisfied there, his hope would immediately leap forward. In the meantime music and light broke into the room when she entered it, and he had to drag himself almost by force into the fields. Once there he worked desperately, to quiet his mind and dispose himself towards sleep, for he slept brokenly. An eternity of silent longing seemed to be before him. His great fear was that he might betray his love by the passionate anger he felt when his stepmother spoke rudely to Anne, or faulted her.

Anne was troubled about Joel. Mrs Widdison was incapable of keeping a secret from her waiting maid. She did not confide in Anne, but she gave her to understand what was happening. Anne knew that Joel's father had a match in prospect for him, and that he was resisting it. She thought that he wished to confide in her, but did not feel it dutiful to his father to do so, for he would linger over chance remarks, and then suddenly jerk himself away. He was heavy-eyed too, and even in this short time he had grown thinner. Her heart ached for him, and she wished often that his grandmother was there still, who would know better than anyone how to comfort him.

One day, in the idle time between Haysel and Harvest, Joel came in early for dinner. He had loitered at a distance from the house, and as he came near it had hurried until he almost ran. He had a picture in his mind of Anne gathering flowers for the table, or whipping up a syllabub in the still-room, or in some way, by some happy chance, alone. He could say something to her, and she would lift up her luminous eyes and answer. He found when he returned, however, that the household was in a bustle. Lady Fettiplace, abroad again after her confinement, had come to spend the day. Ursula was scolding in the kitchen, Jonathon Fletcher was burnishing the silver which Ned had polished, Anne sent twenty ways at once, was hurrying between the dining-room, the still-room and the linen cupboard, called one moment to give out linen, and another to trim the kickshaws or whip up creams. Joel seemed to be in the way. He changed his boots and tidied himself, then went into the Rent Room to read for a while. It was the only quiet room below stairs. After half an hour he judged it time to go into the Withdrawing-Room, where he found Lady Fettiplace, quiet and gentle, sitting with her gentlewoman and Mrs Widdison. It seemed strange that the whole house was in a turmoil about her. She greeted Joel with shy graciousness, and broke off a discussion on raisins of the sun as a part of a baby's diet to ask him if there was any rumour that Dr Fell would be allowed to return to Oxford. Joel answered with an equal shyness and goodwill; but was obliged to say that it did not seem likely as things went at present. Lady

Fettiplace felt that the question had been tactless in that house, for Dr Fell was of the Church party, and hastily asked Mrs Widdison if her gentlewoman had devised any new embroidery.

'I am but started on a pretty little piece of knotted work in white satin,' said Mrs Widdison. 'A spray of flowers in their natural colours, and every one of them grown in our own garden. I should wish your ladyship's opinion on it. It is in the corner. Oh no, it is upstairs.'

She rang the little silver bell at her side.

'My gentlewoman is always where she should not be. Never at hand when she is wanted.'

'Shall I fetch the embroidery frame?' said Joel.

'No, no, you would only be soiling it or scattering the silks. Fetch my gentlewoman. Tell her I want her this instant.'

Joel ran to tell Anne what was wanted, and Lady Fettiplace said deprecatingly, 'There is so much to be done about a house of this size.'

'There are plenty of hands to do it,' said Mrs Widdison. 'But you know how it is with some servants; they had rather do anything than their business.'

Lady Fettiplace had greeted Anne with more pleasure than was tactful, and Mrs Widdison was ruffled, and determined to show that Anne must be kept in her place. Joel returned.

'I have asked Mistress Seckar to fetch the embroidery,' he said.

'I told you to bid her come here,' said his stepmother. 'It is not your business to order my servants.'

Anne came in with the embroidery.

'Why did you not come here directly I sent for you? You have no right to take orders from Master Joel. In future you will listen for my bell, and not go rambling about the house at your own pleasure. Now you will have to go upstairs again, to fetch the – the design you made to work by.'

'Here it is, madam,' said Anne.

'Don't answer back,' said Mrs Widdison. 'Fetch me my other fan, and be quick about it. Run!'

Anne was startled. Mrs Widdison had not spoken so to her for months, and never so in company. She had been well pleased by Lady Fettiplace's visit, and had sent Anne herself to oversee things in the still-room. Something must have happened to vex her. Anne went silently and quickly from the room, but she did not run. Joel's face flamed to the roots of his hair, and he moved abruptly. 'How dare –' he began; but Lady Fettiplace, who had flushed as deeply, checked him with a touch.

'Hush,' she said very softly, 'you will only make it worse.'

Joel bit his lip, and walked to the window.

Mrs Widdison had not observed this short passage, for she felt a familiar, but peculiarly sharp, twinge in her leg. She put her hand quickly to it, and the other leg was similarly affected. As soon as she touched that she felt the pain in her first leg again, slightly higher, and then again in the second. She rubbed the place gently.

'Does not your ladyship find this place very rheumatic?' she said.

'I have not noticed it,' said Lady Fettiplace briefly.

'I am a sad martyr to it,' said Mrs Widdison.

There was silence till Anne returned with the fan.

'That wasn't the one I wanted,' said Mrs Widdison, 'but it will do. Go and get on with your work.'

When Anne had left the room the silence became more palpable, and it was plain to Mrs Widdison that she had behaved without gentility. She fought against the conviction.

'When your ladyship has had the experience of managing a household that I have had,' she said, 'you will learn that it does not do to allow any servant to presume upon your kindness. That girl, for instance, I have raised her almost from the gutter. She was in the utmost need, and could find none to employ her till I took pity on her; and yet if she is not often checked she behaves like a daughter of the house. Confidence soon breeds presumption.'

The sounding phrase fell on the air without response. Lady Fettiplace said nothing; Joel was silent. Presently the gentlewoman began nervously to admire the embroidery, and the conversation was resumed, but sparsely, and it was relief to all when Jonathon Fletcher came to announce dinner. As Joel stood aside to let the last of the ladies, the gentlewoman, pass, he felt as if something tugged at the skirts of his coat. He looked down and saw nothing, but heard, or imagined he heard, a piping but whispered voice; it might have been the starlings on the eaves outside, but that it seemed to come from the level of his knees and to be using articulate words: '*Her*, tell *her*; she's the one as can help.'

Twenty

Well, in absence this will die;
Leave to see and leave to wonder,
Absence sure will help, if I
Can learn how myself to sunder
From what in my heart doth lie.

PHILIP SIDNEY

LADY FETTIPLACE did not stay so long after dinner as she had at first intended. The meal was formal and the conversation stilted. At earlier visits there had been an alacrity, an eagerness, a delight about the hostess which had generated a feeling of comfort, even if it was an alien comfort. That delight had been nipped, and guest and hostess looked bleakly at each other above the flow of formal civilities. The afternoon of music and embroidery and conversation was cut short. Mrs Widdison stood curtseying deeply at the door while Joel handed Lady Fettiplace towards her coach. As he did so he said in a low tone, 'My lady, may I see you alone, to ask your counsel on something that is perplexing me?'

Lady Fettiplace looked startled for a moment, then quickly said, 'I walk in the gardens in the afternoon if you would care to wait on me tomorrow.'

This passed almost in the time of Mrs Widdison's curtsey. Arrived at the coach Lady Fettiplace turned to give thanks for her entertainment with the slighter curtsey which befitted her rank. The coach door was slammed, the heavy coach rumbled into motion and Mrs Widdison turned slowly from the entrance, mounted the stairs at a stately pace and then ran to her bedroom, where she slammed the door and burst into tears. She well deserved those blue marks on her thighs; but it is possible that she was learning something – a little and slowly, for she was not capable of much, but something, at least. Outside the rain splashed down in great drops, and the thunder crashed in a sudden, sharp storm that caught the Fettiplace coach before it reached Swinbrook.

It was fine and warm again next day, however, as Joel walked across the fields to inquire if Lady Fettiplace had suffered no inconvenience from the storm. He had asked his stepmother if he should do so, and she, eager to keep up friendly relations with the great house, had assented readily. The Swinbrook gardens reached almost to the chapel in the fields, so that Joel walked across in a few minutes. Lady Fettiplace was taking the air in her garden, as she had said. Her gentlewoman was picking clove gilli-flowers to dry for pot-pourri, and her nurse was walking beside her, carrying the stiff, swathed-up bundle that contained her baby.

She reassured Joel as to her safety.

'But it is still thunderous, I think,' she said. 'It is so very hot. Mary, don't tire yourself any longer by stooping over those gilli-flowers. Take what you have and spread them out to dry. And take little Edmund in, nurse; this veiled heat is more dangerous than the sun. Come and shelter in the arbour for a short time, Mr Widdison. You look hot after your walk across the fields.'

Joel led her to the gazebo which overlooked the Widford fields with a better grace than he could have shown a few months before.

'I must thank you first, my lady,' he said, 'that you restrained me from speaking yesterday. I was very angry, and I live in dread that an outburst from me may bring trouble on Mistress Seckar.'

'If I am right it is about her that you want to ask my counsel,' said Lady Fettiplace.

'Yes. I beg your pardon if I seem to thrust my affairs on you, but I know that you are a true friend to Mistress Seckar, and now that my Grandmother is dead she has no other.' He paused. 'It is difficult to say,' he said, 'because I have never said it to anyone else. I love her. I love her like – like breath.'

'Do you mean that she loves you in return?'

'I don't know. I don't see how she could. She's different from us. But I couldn't ask her, because she would think it her duty to tell my stepmother, and then she would be harshly treated and sent away. And I don't know if I shall be able to contain myself for ever. The worst is my father has another match in mind for me, and I can't accept it; but it seems so perverse to refuse for ever without a reason, so loving and careful of me as my father is. I should like to tell him; but it would be to her harm, and it would seem folly to him because she has no money, and to her because I am no gentleman.'

Lady Fettiplace pondered. Her first impulse was to disapprove of such a match for Anne. The son of a city merchant, and a Puritan at that, was no mate for the last of the Seckars. It was not as if the Widdisons belonged to one of the great trading houses like Lord Craven; he was one of the vulgar, and his wife was worse, because more pretentious. And yet what lay before Anne if this was refused for her? And the boy was gentle and unpretending, unlike any of his kin. She spoke with hesitation.

'I think, by your own account, you were best to conquer this desire. You do not know that Mistress Seckar has any inclination to you, and you know that your father has other plans. I must tell you frankly that I have urged Mistress Seckar to leave Widford and come and live with me; and she has refused, because she was brought up in the place as a child, and she loves it still. I think that now it would be better for me to ask her again, and more urgently. Once she was away it would be easier for you to put this out of your mind.'

'I shall never forget it,' said Joel. 'But it would be safer and happier for her with you; and if she were away I could tell my father without injuring her.'

He paled at the thought of losing Anne, but a faint hope whispered in his heart that at least he could court her with honour. 'And if she still refuses, my lady, and afterwards things come to a head, and it is impossible for her to stay, you will be willing to receive her?'

'Indeed I shall,' she answered. 'But I pray you do your best to overcome this fancy.'

'I cannot do that,' said Joel, 'but I will do my best to hide it.'

He bowed over her hand, and let himself out at the wrought-iron gate near the chapel. Hobberdy Dick swung himself down from a clump of ivy on the Widford side of the wall, and sat down on one of the stones to meditate. The Fettiplaces were well enough, but they had no call to take Anne away from Widford. It seemed to him that it was time that he bore a hand in the matter.

Twenty-one

He who lies at the wall
Shall have the gold ball;
He who lies at the stock
Shall have the gold rock;
He who lies in the middle
Shall have the gold fiddle.

AFTER long pondering Dick came to the conclusion
that the crux of the matter, to Mr Widdison at least,
was money – gold, that strange magical stuff, so illu-
sory yet so heavy, that could anchor human souls to
earth, that hobs and their like were set to guard; which,
if it were ancient enough, drew even the fairies to the
hollow hills where it lay. Dick knew where the Culver
money was hidden, and Anne Seckar had the right to
it if any living soul still had it; yet it went against his
instincts to betray what had been entrusted to him.
Master Richard had bid him guard it when he rode
away to Towton Field, and it seemed hardly physically
possible to tell that secret to any human ears. He
racked his brains for a solution. Again and again he
approached Anne as she slept and tried to whisper to
her, but found himself tongue-tied. Anne's sleep began
to be broken with dreams of frustration, so that she set
herself to discover what duty it was that eluded her
memory. It seemed, however, as if she was missing
something that had once been hers. At last she thought
that it was Joel's friendship she was missing, and with
that solution it came to her that it was more than
friendship that she felt for him. It seemed to her, as she
went back over their meetings that she had loved him

since the moment when she had looked up from watching beside his grandmother's body and had seen him come into the room, so desolate and so young. The tenderness of love made him seem painfully vulnerable in an insensitive world; yet she had seen strength in him too, truth, and a steady courage at the last resort. Since then they had met only by snatches, but their minds had seemed from the first open to each other, and each short passage between them had had a depth and fullness independent of its duration. Her heart throbbed with the happy certainty that their love was mutual, and then grew cold as she thought how impossible it was of fruition. Such a match would never be allowed; Joel would only fall into endless trouble if he suggested it. Indeed the trouble had already begun in this match, which would be as repellent to him as such a thing would be to her. She was not tormented by any doubt of his love, she realized now that she had looked into his heart too clearly for that; the torment was that she felt the love to be in vain. The only thing that she could do for him was to go away. Swinbrook Manor was not far, but it was another household, where they might be, if they would, as far removed as if they had been in another world.

Dick little knew what turn her thoughts were taking. He continued to beat his brains for some way to give her a clue to the treasure, and never imagined that his activities could stir her up to leave Widford. One difficulty was that Anne was at no leisure to follow any hints he might give her. She had no time by day for straying across to the stableyard, and her heart was too deeply engaged by love and sorrow to leave room for thoughts of gold. He gradually hammered out the notion that Martha might be the one to help. If Mother Darke had tried to raise him to gain the Culver treasure, and it seemed most likely that she had, then she would have partly sensitized Martha's mind to treasure trove. In any case she was the person most easily approached in all the house. He left Anne's bedroom at night and went to the children's, where he started to tell Martha old tales of treasure trove as she slept. In the morning he knew that he had had some success, for he heard her singing as she dressed:

> 'He who lies at the wall
> Shall have the gold ball;
> He who lies at the stock
> Shall have the gold rock;
> He who lies in the middle
> Shall have the gold fiddle.'

'Martha, you know you shouldn't sing such songs of a Sunday morning,' said Rachel primly.

'Was I singing?' said Martha. 'I had such a dream, Rachel. I dreamt that you and me and little Dill went into the stable of a moonlight night, and Anne was there, and her said, "Come down the silver stair." And the moon was shining on the cobbles till it shone them right away, and there was a stair down, and us went down all four, and there was a room all shining with gold, and there was great golden treasures lying here and there; and Anne said, " 'Tis all mine, so pick everyone which you choose." So little Dill her picked up a golden ball, all bright and shining, and you picked up a staff of gold, and 'twas carved all over, and you said, "I'm Queen now," and I picked up a golden fiddle that played of itself so that I didn't never need to learn; and it began to play, and I waked up. And it came back into my head as I was dressing, and it came into my mind that that was how us was lying in bed, just as it says in the rhyme.'

'You do have powerful silly dreams,' said Rachel. 'If I dreamed I'd dream of something better than that.' But Diligence said, 'Tell us some more dreams, Martha, do! Just like that but different.'

Here their mother called them impatiently to come down to prayers, and there was no more time for conversation; but Dick was well satisfied with his success so far. He would have been less pleased, however, if he had seen the letter which Anne had written, against the grain and with hardly restrained tears, during the night.

Anne took the letter with her to church; but the Fettiplaces had ridden over to Chastleton for the week-end, where Prayer Book services were still read secretly, and she had no opportunity to deliver it. There was no need, however. On Tuesday Lady Fettiplace rode over to visit Mrs Widdison. She was dressed with unusual finery, and had armoured herself with an air of sophistication which sat strangely on her.

Mrs Widdison was relieved to see her, though uneasy in her presence after their unspoken difference. As they sat drinking wine together Lady Fettiplace said, 'Oh, I have a small favour to ask you. One of my Wenman cousins is unwell, and has asked me to send my gentlewoman, Mistress Felton, to her, since they are distantly akin. I know from what you said the other day that you do not find Mistress Seckar altogether harmonious. Perhaps it would relieve you from an embarrassment, as well as obliging me, if you would allow me to beg her from you. You are too considerate, I am sure, to turn her out into the world unprovided for, and since you find her unsuited to you you must be in something of a dilemma.'

If Mrs Widdison had not been so before she was now. She had grown dependent upon Anne for the whole running of the household. At the same time pride forbade her to announce it, or to go back on her former declaration. Pride tore her the other way too, for it would have been a grand thing to be able to refuse something that the Fettiplaces wanted. On the other hand, Lady Fettiplace had been kind and friendly, and she had been proud of her acquaintance – a refusal would break it, and probably Anne would be tempted away just the same. No doubt it would be best to yield her with a good grace.

'Of course if your ladyship needs her,' she said, 'my convenience must bow to yours. I have found her useful in many ways; though, as I warned your ladyship, apt to take too much on her. But if you keep a firm hand over her no doubt she will be of service to you.'

She rang her little hand bell, and Ned came, for Anne was busy preparing a dinner in case Lady Fettiplace would stay.

'Bid my gentlewoman come,' she said.

Anne found time to slip the letter into her pocket before she came, a little doubtful in what mood she would find Mrs Widdison.

'Mistress Seckar,' said Lady Fettiplace, 'Mrs Widdison has been kind enough to say that you may come to me, if you will. Mistress Felton is leaving me for a time, and I shall be glad of your company.'

'Yes,' said Mrs Widdison, 'I have been able, to a certain extent, to tell my lady that you are capable of being useful to her. The training that you have received in this house will stand you in good stead, but of course my lady won't expect the familiar ways to which we have been perhaps too lenient here.'

Anne curtsied silently, with her eyes cast down.

'May I send for her then on the day after tomorrow?'

said Lady Fettiplace. 'If you are willing to come, Mistress Seckar?'

'Yes, my lady,' said Anne. 'If I can be spared so soon.'

'It is short notice to seek another gentlewoman,' said Mrs Widdison, 'but no doubt I can make shift.'

'You are more than kind,' said Lady Fettiplace.

She rose, now that her errand was discharged; but accepted Mrs Widdison's invitation to spend a day with her in the next week; for she felt that she owed her some complaisance.

As they rose from their farewell curtsey, Mrs Widdison's eyes met Anne's, and she was touched to see that there were tears in them.

'You will be sorry to leave us, I know,' she said. 'But it is best for you in the long run, though of course you cannot look to meet at Lady Fettiplace's with the indulgence you have had here.'

Anne blushed, and curtsied silently. There seemed nothing to say, and her voice was too unsteady to be trusted. Dick stared at them in incredulous dismay. So this was what Lady Fettiplace's help amounted to! He had been so sure that his advice to Joel was good; the impulse to speak to him had come on a waft that he had long trusted. And now Anne was to go, and Joel would soon be back at Oxford. Widford would be a desolation. Dick felt himself almost ready to leave it, and go with Anne to Swinbrook, but he could hardly press in there when the place was already tenanted, and by an uncongenial spirit like the Abbey Lubber. He tried to console himself by the thought that Anne would be more at her ease among her own people; but, however congenial Lady Fettiplace might be, that restless spirit would make the house unsuitable to her; he had no wish for her to live in a place ordained to destruction. In the meantime, with a heavy heart, he set himself to help Anne in the many tasks which lay between her and her departure.

Anne needed his help, for every step that took her away from Widford seemed a deadly effort; her usual orderly deftness forsook her, and she continually forgot what she had set out to do. The children hung around her as she went about her work, and further impeded her. George Batchford was sullen with annoyance, Charity went about with red eyes and no one echoed old Ursula's sentiment, 'Not before 'twas time.'

Anne had dreaded Joel's reception of the news; but it was something of a surprise to her. He heard it when he came in to dinner. His face whitened, but a glow lit in his eye, and he said quietly, ''Twill be more fitting,' and said no more. Dick was a little cheered by this, for he felt that Joel had some plan in his head; and indeed Joel sat up late, writing and re-writing a letter to his father. Dick sat by him until it was sealed and ready to be dispatched, and then went upstairs to the children's room to continue his work on Martha.

That night he did no more than sit by her pillow crooning gently –

> He who lies by the wall
> Shall have the gold ball;
> He who lies by the stock
> Shall have the gold rock;
> He who lies in the middle
> Shall have the gold fiddle.

He went on tirelessly at it for the greater part of the night, and it rang in Martha's head all the next day.

After two days of continuous activity everything was ready for Anne to go. Preserves had been labelled and wine re-bottled, Mrs Widdison's clothes were all in apple-pie order and the children's work was set to rights. Anne had had little time to prepare her own things, but fortunately they were few, and when she ran up to her attic she found her bundle already tied up, and smelling sweetly of the sprigs of rosemary which had been stuck in among the linen. She knelt down by the bed for a minute, and then looked round the little room. She said under her breath, 'Good-bye, dear Hobberdy Dick,' and ran downstairs to look for a moment into Mrs Dimbleby's empty room. The coach was already at the door, and Lady Fettiplace, drinking wine with Mrs Widdison, heard a confused sound of leave-taking in the hall. In a moment Anne came into the room, ready dressed. Lady Fettiplace judged it best not to extend the time of leave-taking, and rose quickly. The hall was empty when they went out, but everyone in the household had snatched some time to say farewell. Everyone but the most important; Joel was at work in the fields, and neither then nor that morning had he said a word of valediction.

Twenty-two

It was told me I should be rich by the fairies.

Winter's Tale

IT was not till the next Monday that Joel found means to send his letter to his father. It went with his weekly report, for he missed one messenger on Friday, and on Saturday no one was setting out for London. In those days matters went as ill within doors as might be. Outside things prospered well enough, but indoors the history of those days from Thursday to Wednesday was one long catalogue of spills, breakages and recriminations. The milk curdled as it boiled, soot fell from the chimney into the pot, long winding sheets grew on the candles and they burned blue, nothing was ever where it was looked for, the embroidery silks were hopelessly tangled, needles, scissors and bobbins were always astray. The only person whose things were in order was Martha, who at other times was generally in trouble for her disorderly ways, and unfortunately this immunity did her no good, for her mother suspected her of playing practical jokes upon the rest. This was particularly annoying for Hobberdy Dick, for poor Martha was punished by extra work, and had no opportunity to go over to the stable, as she was continually urged to do in her dreams. It was little benefit that her task-work progressed wonderfully, for her mother put more upon her, and was indeed glad of her needle to make up for the loss of Anne's.

Mrs Widdison was puzzled to think how the household could have fallen into disorder so rapidly. There was the matter of her own wardrobe. On Friday morning she had gone over her clothes and found everything in exquisite order, but by Saturday it appeared to be a chaos. It was not that things were thrown down or trampled as if thieves had been at work, but any particular thing she wanted was always at the bottom of everything else, and often torn or spotted besides.

Mrs Widdison began to suspect that Anne had some friend in the household who was doing this in spite; Maria Parminter was persuaded that the house was overlooked, and that the rest of Mother Darke's coven were revenging themselves for the prosecution against her, and old Ursula was gradually coming over to her opinion; George Batchford and Charity were certain they knew how things went. 'Nor yet things won't be straight,' said George Batchford, 'till the young mistress comes back where her should be.'

Everything seemed so undependable that Mrs Widdison looked forward to Wednesday, when Lady Fettiplace was to visit her, with some dismay. Their misfortune, however, seemed rather to abate on Wednesday. The house was by no means in its usual order when Lady Fettiplace arrived, but there had been no disasters in the cooking, nothing was spilled or burned, and for that the household was thankful; for though their ill luck had started only on Friday evening they felt already as if they had never eaten anything but burnt or tainted food in their lives. To the disappointment of most of the household, even of Mrs Widdison, Lady Fettiplace came alone. The children were hanging about the door when she arrived, and Joel, dressed in his Sunday clothes, was talking to Ned about nailing up some of the fruit trees on the front of the house. Martha turned away towards the stables with little

Samuel; but Joel came to hand Lady Fettiplace out of her coach. At the door he paused.

'Will you give me a message for Mistress Seckar,' he said. 'Something you have forgot.'

She looked at him in surprise; he seemed so much older and more self-possessed than when he had last spoken to her.

'I have written to my father,' he said.

Lady Fettiplace was still troubled and undecided, but his steady eye over-bore her.

'Would you ask Mistress Seckar,' she said, 'if she would be so good as to let me have the tracery for the cushion I am to embroider. I should be glad to let Mrs Widdison see it.'

Joel bowed, and walked away towards Swinbrook. Dick, who had been on the point of going with Martha to the stable, turned aside and followed Joel over the field path. He hoped that they would talk together in the garden.

His hope was fulfilled. Joel, holding the pricked tracery in his hand, paced silently with Anne by his side to the gazebo where he had talked with Lady Fettiplace some fortnight before. He handed her to the seat.

'I cannot stay long,' said Anne. 'What is it that you want to tell me?'

'This is the place,' said Joel, 'where I told Lady Fettiplace that I loved you, and asked her help.' He knelt down and took both her hands.

'Dear, dear Anne Seckar, my little mistress, the little mistress of us all, I love you more than all the world beside. Let me tell you so now, when my love can no longer injure you.'

Anne bent her head over this, and cried so that she could not speak.

'Do you love me a little? Even only a little?' cried Joel with mounting hope. She nodded her drooping head, a short nod, and struggled for composure. Joel would have taken her in his arms, but she pressed him back and shook her head.

'Your father –' she said.

'I have written to him. I would not come until I had written, nor speak to you nor look at you until I could do so with honour.'

She smiled at him, and wiped her eyes.

'You are good,' she said. 'I could trust anything to you. But your father would never consent to our marriage. It would only be endless trouble and sorrow for you both, for you are very dear to him, and he to you. Let us each thank God to have known the other, and count each other as dead. That is why I went away.'

'I know my father will not consent at first,' said Joel. 'But if we are steady and patient and dutiful he will consent in the end. Yet, Anne, it may be asking you to wait for a long time. You who are fit to marry anyone.'

'I never could marry anyone else, however long I lived.'

'Then you will keep this ring for me?' said Joel, shyly and eagerly. 'It is worth little in money, but it is the betrothal ring my father gave to my mother. He was poorer in those days.'

It was a silver posy ring, brightly polished, for Joel had lived in the hope of giving it to Anne, and engraved round it was 'Love me and leave me not'. Anne drew out a ribbon from round her neck, and untied a ring from it.

'That shall go in the place of this,' she said. 'It was my mother's betrothal ring too, and is the only Seckar thing I still have.'

'It is as much more precious than mine as you are

than me,' said Joel. 'But if I would take you, why should I boggle at your gear?'

As Anne tied his ring on to the ribbon he examined hers.

'It has a little dove in pearl with something in its beak.'

'My mother was a Culver,' said Anne, 'and it is the dry twig of the Seckars that it is carrying. Seckars and Culvers, we have been so intertwined for generations that we can hardly tell which is which. If you look inside at the back of the dove you will see our arms impaled.'

Joel looked within the ring; then he kissed it; Anne cut loose one of her points, and he hung the ring by it round his neck. Then they rose, and shyly and solemnly kissed each other on the lips, and parted without more words. Joel carried the tracery back with him across the fields, while Dick turned cartwheels behind him, making a strange flurry in the rank, reedy grass of the water meadows.

In the meantime Martha had wandered disconsolately over to the stables. She had counted on seeing Anne that day, though what permanent good it would do her she had not considered. George Batchford was out at work on the farm with the two cart horses; only the saddle horse was standing in its stall. Samuel took a handful of corn from the bin and went to feed him, and Martha scrambled on to the saddle-block which stood in the empty manger under Dick's beam. This was the oldest part of the stable, which had been added to in Elizabeth's reign. George Batchford's loft was above the newer part; but this was unceiled, and a ray of sunlight came down from a small, unglazed window, touched the piece of string by which Dick's kissing ring had been suspended, and slid down in a widening shaft until it struck on the old wood at the foot of the manger. Martha stared at it absently for a moment, and then jumped down from the block. Between the cobbles and the wood there was a narrow line of freshly turned earth, as if a row of cobbles had just been lifted, but it was not that that caught her eye at first. On the hoary old wood, just where the ray of sunlight struck, there was the rough outline of a fiddle.

Martha stared at it incredulously for a moment, and then called to Samuel, 'Sam! Sam! Come here quick!' Sam squeezed out of the manger and ran to her. 'Do you see that fiddle there?' said Martha.

'Fiddle,' said Sam, recognizing it instantly.

'That's the picture of my golden fiddle,' said Martha. 'And depend on it, Sam, the gate to our silver stair's hidden somewhere here, if so be as we know how to find it.'

Forgetting in her excitement that she was in her Sunday best for Lady Fettiplace's visit, Martha ran across the yard to find a spade. The heavy muck shovel was leaning against the wall, and she tried that first, but it was too wide to fit into the narrow space between the cobbles and the wood. The pointed trenching spade would be best, but George had carried that with him to the fields. She found a heavy garden spade and a mortar trowel. The spade was almost too much for her; but she started to try to dig out the loose earth with it, while Samuel seized gladly upon the trowel, and squatted on the cobbles to scoop up the soil, the satin skirts of his long coat spread out behind him in the dirt of the stable. They dug for some time but made little way, for the gap was too narrow to allow much purchase on the spade, and Martha had to scoop out the loosened soil with her hands. She had begun to hope, however, that she was coming to an empty space under the manger when there was a sound of feet in the yard, and Maria Parminter stood breathless in the doorway.

'Dear sakes!' she exclaimed. 'You'll be in a peck of trouble and no mistake. The dinner's on the table and Joan Naismith looking everywhere for Samuel.' She snatched him by the arm. 'You naughty boy, to get yourself into such a pickle!' she said, slapping him. 'His new dove-coloured satin and all. I would not wonder if Joan lost her place for this.'

''Twas my fault,' said Martha. 'Don't cry, Sammy.' She put an arm round him.

'Watch the skirts of your dress,' said Maria Parminter. 'They're near as bad as his, only he's wiped his hands all down his front. I'll take him in to Joan to be changed, and tell the mistress he had a fall in the yard; and do you wash your face under the pump and come in so quick as you can, and maybe she'll not notice the hem of your frock till you have time to clean it.' She picked Samuel up under her arm, and hurried towards the house. Martha took time to seize an armful of straw and scatter it over the newly turned earth; then she wetted her handkerchief at the pump and wiped her face clean. Hobberdy Dick only joined her then, for Joel had come home but just in time for dinner. He turned back into the stable to hide the traces of her work more thoroughly, while Martha went with an apprehensive heart into the house.

It may be imagined that her reception was unfavourable, though Maria Parminter had made the best gloss upon the matter that she could. Both Joel and Lady Fettiplace pleaded for her, but her behaviour looked so like wanton naughtiness that Mrs Widdison's anger might be excused. Her 'Go to your room. Ursula, see to it', gave them little ground to go upon.

Ursula saw to it with a heavy hand; and, what Martha minded even more, she locked her in the west attic, empty since Anne's departure, and safe from intercourse with the outside world. It was almost more than she could bear to be prevented from pursuing her researches; and she had left the place dreadfully open to alien discovery. Her only comfort was that the stable was George Batchford's domain. He was to be trusted, she knew. If she could only tell him, he would guard her secret, and not look until she was there to look with him. The worst of it was that the west attic was on the opposite end of the house to the stable, and George was unlikely to come round the front of the house as he returned from the fields. Nevertheless Martha pulled the stool under the window and stood on it, looking out in the hope that she might see him. She was only once interrupted, by old Ursula, who limped in, more than usually lame, with some bread and water. Charity had offered to bring it, but Ursula knew better than to trust any of the maids where Martha was concerned. Her slow approach gave Martha time to scramble off the stool and sit down upon it. She ate and drank, for she was hungry and very thirsty; but as soon as she had finished she climbed up on to the stool again, and resumed her watch. It lasted a long time, but at last her patience was rewarded. It was getting on for milking time when Daisy, usually as quiet a cow as need be, came charging stiffly round the corner of the house into the garden, with her tail up as if she had the breeze. Once there, however, she halted and began to snatch at the roses. George Batchford and Charity came round the house after her. Charity was the friendliest of the maids, and Martha was not afraid to trust her.

'George! George Batchford!' she called. 'I'd dearly

love to have a tell with 'ee. 'Tis something as won't wait.'

George Batchford looked cautiously along the front of the house, and then nodded.

'Wait till 'tis dark,' he said, 'and us'll see.'

Martha got off her stool and lay down on the pallet to wait till darkness with what patience she could command. It was well for her that the ghost had been laid, for her mother did not send for her, nor did old Ursula visit her again that night. Her mother's heart was yearning a little over her; but the sight of Samuel's new satin dress hardened her in her anger, and Martha had been so often in disgrace lately that this final offence seemed especially wanton. Joel, whose heart was more than usually tender that day, had no success in persuading his stepmother to forgiveness, and felt in the end that he had perhaps made things worse for Martha. He determined that he would find some way of alleviating her punishment on the morrow. The Lacys of Shipton had invited him to supper that night, and it struck him that if he could return with an invitation to his stepmother it might make things pleasanter for Martha. He therefore excused himself, and set off as the dusk was falling. Martha did not hear him go, for by this time she was fast asleep, tired with the excitements of the day.

Martha slept till she was awakened by a grating sound at her window, and saw the moonlight darkened by George Batchford's head. She tiptoed across the room to him in her stockinged feet.

'I hope 'tis summat of import you were minded to say,' said George Batchford. 'For here I am risking the neck of me on a couple of ramshackle ladders.'

Martha thrust out her head and whispered, 'Oh 'tis ever so important, George. Listen now.' She told him the whole story of the dream and the fiddle newly drawn on the manger, and the row of cobbles that had been lifted.

''Tis the Culver gold right enough,' said George Batchford. 'And 'tis you as is meant to find it. If I come back in two hours or three when the house is asleep would you be afraid to wriggle through the window and climb down with me? I dursen't lift the treasure without you, and that's the truth.'

'But 'tis Anne's money,' said Martha. 'That's what my dream said.'

'And it said true,' said George Batchford.

'Seek Eastward and Westward wherever you please,
The Seckars and Culvers are like as two peas.

They say there's no Culver now, for the last of them died of the plague in Bristol, so Mistress Seckar's the last of the old stock, and fitting it is that the money should come to her. Do you think this window is too small for you?'

'I can get through it right enough. Do you tell Joel, and he'll come and help us.'

'Master Joel is out. If so be he comes back he'll come to the stable, and us can tell him easily enough. Here's a slice of bread and a bit of cheese Charity sent up to you. She was main vexed that old she-bear wouldn't let her carry up your dinner. 'Twould have been better fare if her had, so 'twould.'

'Thank you, George,' said Martha, and sat down thankfully to eat her supper, while George went cautiously down the ladder.

The time went even more slowly now, for Martha's pulses were throbbing with excitement; but at length she heard the maids coming upstairs to bed. Soon the laughter and talking ceased, and they fell silent. Not long after she heard George's cautious step on the ladder, and she hurried to her stool. It was no easy matter to wriggle through that small window, and turn so as to set her feet on the ladder, the more difficult since she was below the level of the window to begin with. After several attempts George hauled her up to the window, she put her arms round his neck and he climbed to the topmost rung of the ladder, with his hands on the gable ends, while she scrambled up and out. Then she turned cautiously round towards the house, and they went down the ladder together. George took it down, for fear Joel might see it, and raise an alarm of thieves before he knew what was going on.

'Us'll borrow the key from old Ursula when her's once sound asleep, and put you in that way,' said George. 'The young Master's not back; but Charity's offered to sit up and let Fletcher go to bed, so all's safe there. Her'll come out and lend us a hand. I'll go surety for she. I'd not tell another, unless it might be the young mistress, but I've an eye to Charity, for so young as she is, and so soon as I can save up for the plenishings of a house her and me will be wed.'

'Oh, George, I'm glad on it!' said Martha. 'For Charity's nothing but the street to look to if old Ursula got her turned away, and she's as good as gold.'

'That her is,' said George heartily, 'And a prettyish enough girl, if so be as her is smartened up.'

They had reached the back door by this time, and lifted the latch cautiously. Charity was kindling a candle lantern from her dip. She put a finger to her lip, and glanced to the corner behind the settle where Jonathon Fletcher and Ned were asleep on their pallets. She picked up a wooden beaker of milk from the dresser, and offered it to Martha when they reached the scullery. Martha took a draught from it, but was too much excited to pause, and carried it with her to the stable. She saw that George had everything ready to begin work. The straw had been raked back from the digging, and the trenching spade and trowel were at hand. It was a very different matter when George was there. He soon had a narrow trench that stretched the length of the manger.

'Put thy hand in there, Martha,' he said, 'just below the picture of the fiddle.'

Martha did so, and groped about in the dark behind the woodwork.

'Seems to me,' she said, 'like there's a handle that ought to turn, but 'tis terrible stiff.'

'I'll dig round a bit and get my arm in,' said George. 'Ah, here 'tis. 'Tis stiff, right enough. Ah, when that's turned seems as if the whole panel will lift. Give us a hand Charity.'

Between them they pulled the old wood of the manger forward, and under and behind the manger they saw a cupboard cut out of the thickness of the wall. It had been well concealed by a row of cobbles, and secured by a catch besides. Martha shone the lantern into it, and they saw an old and heavy chest, banded with iron. It was so heavy that George alone could not move it. He and Charity took hold of the handle at each end, and pulled it forward to the front of the cupboard, but could not lift it over the narrow trench. Martha, however, put her small hands in to help, and they got it out more easily than they had expected. There it lay, solid, dirty and forbidding before them, and Martha had time to regret the silver stair of her dream, and the gleaming golden treasure in the great treasure room. This was different indeed; but she did not regret it long, for she was in love with facts.

'Well here 'tis,' said George Batchford in a low voice. 'There's the Culver gold in there. But where's the key? Is there a deeper cupboard, or has Mistress Seckar any knowledge of where to find it?'

A little shower of mortar fell trickling into the manger, and Martha cried, 'I know in my heart where 'tis, George. Make a stiff arm, and lift me up so high as you can, the way I can reach the rafters.'

She stiffened herself and held her breath, and George grasped her by the ankles and slowly raised himself. She held by his arms until she was right above his head, and then reached up quickly for the rafters. She swung herself along them, steadied by George's hands, until she came to where they met the joists, near where Dick's kissing ring used to hang. She felt along the ledge, and there, pushed well back, she found a great, heavy key.

'Here 'tis, George,' she cried triumphantly.

The key had all the air of having been recently oiled, and George turned the lock without difficulty. Charity held the lantern low, and they all stooped forward eagerly to see the heavy leather bags and the silver mazers and cups, all blackened with tarnish, which were stored tightly in the chest. It was as different as possible from the shining treasure of Martha's dreams.

They had all been so absorbed till now that not one of them, not Dick himself, had heard any noises outside the stable. Now they heard the stamping of horse's hoofs over the cobbles.

''Tis Joel come back just in time to see it!' said Martha. 'Joel!' And she ran to open the door. At the same time came a flash of lightning and a sharp crack of thunder which almost drowned her voice. Martha tripped as she ran, and fell into the shadow, out of the light of the lantern. At the same time the door opened, and Mr Widdison, weary and bespattered, led a horse into the stable.

Twenty-three

'Me list not' (said the Elfin knight) 'receave
Things offred, till I know it well be got;
Ne wote I but thou didst these goods bereave
From rightfull owner by unrighteous lott,
Or that bloodguiltinesse or guile them blott.'

The Faerie Queene

MR WIDDISON stood still in amazement at the scene
before him, and the others looked at him in no less
surprise. He did not notice Martha as she stood in the
shadows, and his first suspicion was of wantonness at
finding George Batchford and Charity in the stable
together at midnight. But the momentary first picture
formed in his mind had been of them stooping over
something, and he cast his eye down, and saw the great
chest, and the pile of earth and the spades.

'What have we here?' he said. 'What wicked doings
are these?'

'Naught of wickedness,' said George Batchford.
'This here's the Culver gold, that you must have heard
tell of, Master, which have been hid none knows
how long, till the time was ripe for it to be brought to
light.'

Mr Widdison stood still for a moment, and then led
his horse to the manger and carefully tied it up. As he
did so George glanced once or twice from where he
knew Martha was standing to the door, and jerked his
head aside. Martha realized how awkward it would be
for him to explain her presence, and slipped out of the
stable. As she ran across the yard the moon shone out
again from between black clouds, and she saw Joel

riding down the Fulbrook track. She ran towards him.

'Joel, my father is here, and George and I have found the Culver gold that belongs by right to Anne. My father didn't see me there, and 'twas George let me out, so don't tell on him. But, oh, go quick and tell Father that 'tis Anne's and none of ourn.'

Joel had drawn rein as she ran up to him, and after she had left him he sat for a moment with the rein still taut, momentarily stunned by such a weight of information in so small a compass. Then he urged his horse forward, and rode in all haste to the stable.

In the meantime Martha slipped into the house, and stole up the moonlit attic stairs. As she made her way past the maids' beds one of them said sleepily, 'Is that you, Charity?' but she said nothing, and groped for the handle of old Ursula's door. There was nothing for it but to try and steal away the key. As she fumbled, however, her hand encountered metal of another kind, long and uneven. It was the key she wanted. She turned back to the west attic and unlocked the door. The best thing she could think of was to leave the key on the outside, and trust that Charity, or someone else, would lock it and return the key to Ursula's room. She had done what she had set out to do, and had little doubt of the issue. She lay down on the little pallet bed, and fell at once into a sound and dreamless sleep.

Things did not proceed so smoothly in the stable. Mr Widdison fumbled a little as he tied up his horse in an ominous silence. It is not to be wondered at that he was taken aback. To have ridden furiously late into the night to prevent a son from casting himself away on a disastrous match, to arrive forespent and weary at midnight and to find the servants digging up, or burying, treasure at midnight in one's own stable – this is enough to disconcert any man. Wild tales of gangs and robbers came into his head, and he moved over to see if this was indeed ancient treasure or the spoils of the road. The first glance reassured him, and he stooped down to lift one of the leather bags. It came apart with the weight of its contents, and a small pile of ancient gold shone dully in the candle light. Mr Widdison lifted one coin; it was thick and heavy, worth four times as much as a King Charles sovereign. He looked up at them, and his face flushed.

'How did you come on this?' he said. Then, as George Batchford gathered his wits to answer, he said suddenly, 'Didn't I hear Martha's voice as I came in?'

George Batchford looked at him with a face set in blankness.

'That's a strange thing now,' he said. ''Twas a dream of the little maid as set us to look. Indeed her started to dig earlier, and fell into trouble for mucking of her fine clothes, and was sent to bed afore dinner. 'Tis a strange place this, and no mistake.'

Mr Widdison pursued the subject no further, but knelt to examine the contents of the chest. He did not move the bags, but began to count them as they lay. As he did so the clatter of a second horse's hoofs was heard on the cobbles, and he shut down the lid as Joel led the cob into the stable.

'Joel! What are you doing out at this time of night? Is this the order you keep in my absence?'

'I was supping at Shipton Court,' said Joel, 'and Bayard cast a shoe on the way back. I was so lucky as to find a smith working late, and had him re-shod; but it has delayed me. You here, Father! I did not look to see you so soon. What have you there?'

'George Batchford has unearthed a chest of ancient treasure,' said Mr Widdison. 'It is a strange hour to work in, and I don't know what business he had to call Charity into it; but money never comes amiss. You shall have a luck penny from it, both of you, and Martha too if she brought it to light, as you say.'

''Tis the Culver gold, master,' said George Batchford, 'and known to be such to all the countryside.'

'The Culvers can have known naught of it, or they would never have left it,' said Mr Widdison. 'The land is mine and all that stands on it. And so far as I know there is not a Culver left alive to claim it.'

'Mistress Seckar is the last of the Culver blood,' said Joel. 'The Culver treasure belongs of a right to her.'

'The less said on that head, Joel,' said his father, 'the soonest mended. Give me a hand and we'll carry it upstairs to my room. It's not safe to leave it here, for though the iron is strong the wood may well be rotten. I'll have it in safety under my bed, and we'll look at it in the morning.'

It took the three of them, and Charity as well, to lift the heavy box, heavier, it seemed, than ever. They moved stumblingly into the house as if they were carrying a coffin; and Mrs Widdison waked with a scream, as the door of her chamber burst open and they staggered into the room.

'Quiet, Martha,' said Mr Widdison. 'I've something of value here that I can't leave downstairs. I'll tell you about it presently. Get me something to eat, Charity, and some hot water to wash in, for I'm forespent. And, Batchford, wake Jonathon Fletcher and tell him to get me some ale. Joel, you and I will talk in the morning.'

He took off his coat, and the rest went out of the room.

''Tis sheer robbery and nothing else,' said George

Batchford. 'It belongs to the little mistress by rights, and if any other meddles with it he'll have to reckon with me.'

'Wait till morning,' said Joel. 'My father is an honest man, and he'll give all their rights, when he understands them. He's come on this all of a sudden.'

'Charity,' said George Batchford, 'run and see that little Martha is safe locked in. Get her key out of the old she-bear's room, and put it back there; and if so be you waken her, say the Master's home and needs food and firing. Well, we'll wait till morning, master, for there's little other us can do. As you say, the Master's an honest man enough, but he'm terrible slow to see reason, and so stubborn as a badger. But us'll hope for the best.'

Hobberdy Dick agreed with George Batchford; and his experience of human nature led him to think that a good meal and a night's sleep would make Mr Widdison more convincible; but he felt that he might do something to pave the way for Joel's arguments in the morning. He fetched a soft leather from the shelf in the pantry where Jonathon Fletcher kept his cleaning things, and waited until Samuel Widdison was in bed and asleep. Then he went into the best bedroom and under the bed. The ghost was there already, drawn by the smell of real gold, and was clawing impotently at the chest in vain efforts to open it. Dick drew the key from under Mr Widdison's pillow, and opened the box easily. The ghost immediately slipped inside. It did not take Dick long to do what he had to do; but it took a good deal longer to get the ghost out of the chest again. Dick did not want its plebeian sliminess to pollute the Culver treasure. At length he took one coin out, and gave it to the ghost to play with. It could not lift it, but it patted and stroked it all night, crooning happily, and Samuel Widdison's sleep was the more blessed. Dick locked the chest and returned the key to its place under the pillow. He felt that he had done all he could to prepare against the morrow, and went down to sleep in the embers.

Twenty-four

Jack shall have Jill,
Naught shall go ill;
The man shall have his mare again,
And all shall go well.

A Midsummer Night's Dream

THE two subjects that Joel had to discuss with his
father the next morning were so intertwined that it
seemed a mere chance which of them would come
uppermost. A sleepless night had ill prepared Joel to
deal calmly with either matter, and prayers and breakfast seemed endless to his impatience. But at length
his father had finished, and called Joel into the Rent
Room. Samuel Widdison sat at the table, and Joel
stood in front of him. There was a moment's silence,
and then Mr Widdison took Joel's letter out of his
pocket, and unfolded it.

'I was much distressed and disappointed to receive
this letter from you yesterday,' he said. 'The more so
as you had assured me that your affections were not
engaged. I expected more straightforward dealing from
you than that.'

'I did not know, sir, when I told you so, that I did
love Anne. It was your proposal that opened my own
heart to me. Indeed, sir, there was not a word of love-
making between us until I had writ that letter to you.
I wished above all things to act openly.'

'But there has been since!' said Mr Widdison. 'What
kind of openness is this, to write to me, and hasten
across to commit yourself before I had time to answer

or come? It is out of the question that you should marry a dowerless girl, who has been your mother's servant. Unless you give up all notion of it I must take you away from College, and you must go back to town with me.'

'Father,' said Joel, 'I ask for no present concession from you. Mistress Seckar is not here; as you know she is the Lady Fettiplace's gentlewoman now. The term is starting soon, and I shall see nothing of her. We only ask to be allowed to wait. Sure, sir, when you wedded my mother her dower was small enough.'

'My wealth was not much more then. It is different now. I am a warm man, Joel, and wealth must look to wealth. Nor should I wish you to marry into one of the old malignant families. They are going down in the world, and there is no strength in them.'

'There is strength in Anne, Father,' said Joel proudly. 'The whole house depended on her. You will see what a difference it makes now she is gone. But, sir, may I tell you about the treasure that was found last night. It seems there has always been a rumour that a great store of gold had been hidden by the Culvers in the old days; but it has never been found till now, when George Batchford was led to it. It was he found it; and he feels strongly that it must go to the Culvers or their heirs; and all the countryside will feel with him I know.'

'Why do you think that it has been hid all this time, not to be come at by any of the family, who might have some notion of where it was hid, and been brought to light in the end with the turn of a spade, by a child and two servants that can't so much as spell their own names? Why but that Providence intended it should come to us, and not bolster up one of the old decaying houses?'

'But you can't take another man's goods and call it Providence,' said Joel.

'No man can accuse me of taking what is not mine,' said Mr Widdison. 'In the first place there are no Culvers alive that we know of. You know when I was paying the last of the money we heard how they had all died of the plague in Bristol. So far as we knew there's not a chick nor child of Culver blood alive this day. Secondly, we have no proof that this is Culver gold at all. It may have laid here long before the Culvers were thought of. It looks old enough.'

'Mistress Seckar is the last of the Culver blood, sir,' said Joel.

'So the rumour runs among the servants, and as to blood it may be true enough. But how are we to know she's not a by-blow?'

'You go too far, sir,' said Joel. 'I have seen the Culver arms impaled with the Seckars. As for whether the treasure was buried here before Culver days, we have the title deeds, and we have only to look at the coins to see if they date before Culver times.'

His father admired the readiness and ingenuity of the argument. The thought went through his mind that it might be worth sending the lad to the Inns of Court when he was through College. Legal knowledge was always useful in a city company. He spoke in a gentler tone; though all he said was, 'Unless I had definite proof that the Seckars were already connected with the Culvers when the treasure was hid I should not think it right to part with it on so frivolous a pretext.'

'May we go and look at it, sir?' said Joel.

Samuel Widdison was curious to examine the treasure again, and he rose with alacrity and led the way to the best bedroom, which, to Ursula's annoyance, he had locked that morning. He unlocked it, and locked it behind them again, and he and Joel pulled the great chest out from under the bed. The floor of the bedroom was unrushed, so they could take the money out and range it without fear of losing any. There were twelve bags, one of them represented by the scattered pile which Mr Widdison had left the night before. Mr Widdison picked the others out more carefully, emptied them and began to count the contents, bag by bag. They were mixed, but all ancient. Joel turned his attention to the plate. There was one small cup of gold, but the rest was all silver, black as gunmetal, great flat dishes and cups. In a moment he gave a cry of surprise.

'Look, Father! Look here!' he said. 'Here is the proof you asked for.'

His father turned from his counting, and Joel thrust into his hand a large loving cup, the handles doves with their wings outspread. It was black like the rest, but at one side shone a small spot of burnished silver, where two shields showed side by side. Joel pulled up a ring by a ribbon round his neck.

'Look inside here, sir,' he said. There was no doubt about it; the engraving on the cup was more primitive, but there was the dry twig of the Seckars, side by side with the Culver dove.

Mr Widdison looked, and was convinced. He was an honest man, but money was dear to him; and he piled the gold back into the chest in a bitter silence. Joel helped him with the plate; then he locked the chest again and stood up.

'We must send for Mistress Seckar,' he said. 'You'll find, maybe, she is less ready to mate with you now she has gold as well as birth.'

Joel knew better. He smiled and said nothing.

It was some comfort to Mr Widdison that he had refused to show the contents of the chest to his wife. It saved him a bitter clamour there. They locked the bedroom door behind them again, and went down to the Rent Room. Mr Widdison called for Ned.

'Put a side saddle on Bayard,' he said, 'lead him across the fields to Swinbrook, and deliver a note to my lady Fettiplace. I will have it ready for you by the time the horse is saddled.'

He sat stiffly down to write, for his long ride had galled him, and Joel stood near him in silence. His heart glowed towards his father; for he thought, and with truth, that there were few merchants who could check themselves, and abandon wealth which they counted already theirs without a word of outcry.

Mr Widdison folded the letter and sealed it.

'I have asked my lady Fettiplace,' he said, 'to spare Mistress Seckar to us for half a day on a matter of great concernment to her.'

'Thank you, sir,' said Joel. 'You have done like yourself.'

Mr Widdison sighed sharply. His son's approbation was dear to him; but with a sudden pang he felt how often and how criminally he was dispossessed of the self which Joel commended. Yet Joel was right; this was indeed the central pattern of himself; though he alone knew how unlike it was to his usual thoughts and actions.

Ned went off with the note, while the household seethed with unsatisfied curiosity. All knew something of the chest, for Mrs Widdison knew of it; all knew that the best bedroom was locked, and rumours of the Culver treasure ran round the place, though those that knew most kept silence. Martha was free from her captivity, and on tiptoe to know what would happen next;

but she had no chance to discuss it with George Batchford, who had gone off in glum silence to the fields, nor with Charity, who was too directly under Ursula's eye to be engaged in any private conversation. When Ned was seen to go off towards Swinbrook speculation ran wild, and Martha's hopes rose. Fortunately no one had long to wait. Within three-quarters of an hour Anne was seen riding across the field, with Ned walking behind her. Mr Widdison met her at the door.

'Will you come upstairs?' he said. 'I have something of importance to show you.'

They were the target of almost every eye in the house as he led her up to the best bedroom. Mrs Widdison, watching them from the Drawing Room, was ready to scream with unsatisfied curiosity. It was almost agony to her; but there was something formidable about her husband just then which restrained her questions. Not a word passed between Mr Widdison and Anne until he had locked them into the room, and unlocked the chest. Then he said, 'George Batchford dug up this chest in the stable last night. He and my son maintain that it belongs to you, and these arms prove that they speak truly.'

'The Culver gold!' said Anne. She knelt down beside it and touched it lightly. 'My grandmother used to say that it was hid somewhere about the place; but only one knew where. It's like a tale come true to see it.' She looked up at him. 'But the house is yours now. It was found on your property, and you have the right to it.'

'I should have said so,' he answered, 'if there had been no heir to the Culvers. But these arms prove your right.'

'That would be when Maud Seckar married Reginald Culver,' she said. 'We had more land in those days. Take half of it, sir, you have the right.'

'I have no right to a penny of it,' he answered. 'When George Batchford is back from work, so that we have men enough to guard it, I will send it across the fields to you at Swinbrook.'

'No need to do that,' she said. 'Your son has told you, I know, how it stands with us. When you permit our marriage the money will be his. In the meantime may I put most of it in your hands to trade for me? And the plate must remain here, for it belongs to Widford.'

Samuel Widdison looked at her in delighted admiration. He thought to himself that he had never looked at her before. A little pale, quiet thing, there she stood, as decisive and straightforward as a man, and spoke her mind without a pause or quaver. How fine and small her hands were, and how clear and bright and grey were her eyes! Her whole face kindled till she seemed like a pale flame. Joan Peto would be a washer-woman beside her, dress her how you might. He would think the better of Joel ever after for this choice. But his admiration drove him another step along the path of honesty. He said:

'You should bethink you, and ask my lady Fettiplace for counsel before you leave this gold in my hands. The fortune here may not be great, but it is enough to dower you suitably to your birth. You can look for a better match than Joel now.'

'I couldn't look for a better match than Joel in all the round world,' she said. 'Perhaps you think that we are too young to marry yet; but we will wait for each other until you judge the marriage is fitting. In the meantime I will work for the lady Fettiplace.'

'Joel should go through College,' said Mr Widdison,

'but if I have my way you shall stay here as our future daughter until the time comes for you to wed. Take this key. I will send Joel to you.'

He went downstairs, to send Joel up, and to satisfy his wife's curiosity.

Twenty-five

Seest thou now, Thomas, yonder way
  That lyse low undur yon rise?
Wide is the way, the sothe to say,
  Into the joyes of paradyse.

Thomas and the Fairy Queen

JOEL and Anne talked for a long time together in the best bedroom; or so it seemed to the rest of the household. The time was passed by Hobberdy Dick in frantic attempts to get the servants to concentrate on a suitable dinner to mark the occasion; but his work was in vain, for they never stayed in the kitchen for more than ten minutes on end.

After a while Charity was called away, and Ned was sent to fetch George Batchford from the fields; and these two, with Martha, Joel and Anne, sat down to reconstruct the whole story from the beginning. At the end of it Anne unlocked the chest, and they all examined the treasure together, and burnished the silver as best they could; and then Anne picked one bag out of the chest, took three pieces out of it for Martha, and gave the rest to George Batchford.

'This is yours,' she said, 'as it is only right it should be; and I hope it will go a long way to buy furnishings for your house.'

By that time some kind of a meal had been got together – at least it was neither rancid nor burnt – and after that it was time for Anne to go back to Swinbrook. Joel walked with her across the fields.

'You know whom we owe this to, don't you?' said

Anne. 'Only Hobberdy Dick knew where the treasure was; and how cleverly he set about showing us how to get it! Dear Hobberdy Dick! It is like having a guardian angel in the house.'

Six weeks later Joel rode back from Oxford for his betrothal. Hobberdy Dick had been too light-hearted to make the house as uncomfortable as it had been after Anne first left, but he saw to it that Mrs Widdison missed Anne enough to be very glad to get her back; and indeed Mrs Widdison had been not only uncomfortable but lonely without Anne. There was a companionableness about her that could not but be missed.

The betrothal was a festive occasion; with presents from Lady Fettiplace and the neighbours and the children, with signing of settlements and the exchange of rings. Mr Widdison would not hear of dancing; but George Batchford had Hugh Powell hidden in the stable, and the oast-house was gay with berries and late flowers, as if for a harvest festival.

When Lady Fettiplace had said good-bye to Anne, and gone, Joel and Anne went out into the garden in the dusk to discuss their plans.

'My father means to go back to town in three years or so, when we are married,' said Joel, 'and leave us in charge here. I should like, if you would like it too, that the child of ours who inherits this place should take the name of Seckar. He would have no right to be called Culver, and George Batchford says that Seckars and Culvers are as like as two peas. I think Hobberdy Dick would miss a Seckar about the place after we are gone.'

'You shall settle that as you like,' said Anne. 'It may be that they will not want to part with the name of Widdison. But one thing I should like, Joel, is to beg that Martha should stay with us. She was never made for the town.'

'I think her mother would be glad of it,' said Joel. 'She would think there would be a chance of a good match for her here.'

'There is one thing more I want to ask you, Joel, while we are alone together. Wait here in the arbour, and I will fetch something that I want you to see.'

Joel sat down in the arbour his grandmother had loved to use, and Hobberdy Dick crouched on the ground outside. Their talk of dying had sent a pang through his heart, and he realized that he had never loved human beings as he loved these two. Yet the inexorable time would come when they would float away as all the rest had done, and he would see them no more for ever. Anne came running back, and spread out the things which she had brought for Joel to see. He peered at them in the dusk, and Hobberdy Dick came creeping round to look too.

'All this time when I was at Swinbrook,' said Anne, 'I have been thinking of Hobberdy Dick. He has done so much for us that I cannot see how it can be right not to do something to thank him. So I have made these two suits, one scarlet and one green, the best I could make, and I have made this little broom too; and I thought I would lay them out and let him take his choice.'

'I know little of such things by comparison with you,' said Joel. 'But I have always heard that it is unlucky to give them clothes, or any reward but food.'

'So they say, Joel; but they give all kinds of reasons, and one is this, that — lobs and such as they are doomed to serve men until they have earned a reward, and then they are free to go to happiness. I could not bear to think that we held Hobberdy Dick against his will, so kind as he has been to us. If he wishes to stay with us the broom will give him a choice; and I know he is too kind to take offence at what we offer with such good will. If he goes the house will be empty indeed without him – I cannot tell you what he was to me when first I came – but for all that he has the right to go.'

'If that is how it is, indeed I wouldn't keep him,' said Joel. 'Let us lay them out in the kitchen when the servants are dancing in the oast-house. But if he goes I don't know how we shall face George Batchford.'

He gathered the things carefully up, and they went in to supper, while Dick lingered in the arbour, pendulous between grief and rapture. Presently he wandered along to the bee-hives, and clambered up on to their stands, one after another.

'They be putting out clothes for I,' he whispered to each. The hens had gone to roost, but he crept into the henhouse and stroked his little red hen. For all that he had not yet decided. After that he went into the oast-house, where songs, drinking and speeches were in full swing, but not yet dancing, for Joel and Anne were still with them, and they could not well countenance what Mr Widdison had forbidden. Presently Joel and Anne went out; but Dick still stayed for a little while, until Hugh Powell struck up for the dance. He looked lingeringly round the lighted room. He had seen good days in Widford, and good days were yet to come, though the old oast-house could hardly stand much longer. But he must go to Joel and Anne; they would be laying out his presents. They were just finishing as he went into the kitchen. The hearth was neatly swept, and the fire was burning clearly. A dish of cream stood on the dresser with a piece of betrothal cake beside it. Dick knew the cake well, he had ground the nuts for it, and stoned most of the raisins. The little

broom was propped up against the settle – a peeled
willow haft and fine birch twigs. Anne was laying out
the clothes on a little bench, bright green and a fresh,
clear scarlet. They were made of fine cloths and delicately stitched. She must have worked many hours at
them over at Swinbrook, with the old Abbey Lubber
glooming out of the shadows. Anne spread them carefully and drew back.

'Dear Hobberdy Dick,' she said, 'here is your choice,
spread out with all the goodwill of our hearts. If you
will stay you know how glad we shall be; if you go, our
love go with you. And may the choice be the best to
you, whichever it be.' She took Joel's hand. 'We
mustn't watch him,' she said, 'but let us stay in the
outer kitchen in case he has anything to say to us.'

They went, and Dick drew near the settle, inch by
inch, like a cat stalking. When he was within arm's
reach he made a quick dart at the cream and cake. That
he could take without committing himself; and he carried it to the fireside, and sat down cross-legged on the
hearth, eating and drinking, with his eyes fixed on his
gifts all the while. He rinsed out the cream dish and
put it on the dresser, then returned to the settle, humming mechanically under his breath the hobgoblins'
song of departure. He knew, or almost knew, what each
choice entailed. The broom would mean that his spell
of service would be indefinitely renewed; until some
other mortal was so grateful or so rash as to offer him
freedom again, or until some witch enslaved him, or
some exorcist banished or imprisoned him. He touched
the broom with the tip of one finger, and saw as if in a
vision what his service would be – the happy days
under the Seckars, and then the time when the Fettiplaces took refuge there from their Abbey Lubber, and
built a grand new wing where the stables and oast-

house now stood, and the return of the Seckars again, rich times and poor times, but through it all Widford would be a happy house and well guided. But when Anne and Joel went he would never see them again. He drew back his hand from the broom and looked at the clothes, humming a little louder. He knew well what the green suit meant – his entry to fairyland and the freedom of all the hollow hills in the country. But fairyland was no temptation to him; he had no wish to join that simulated, antic mirth, nor to enjoy those dusty splendours. It was the red suit that drew him; yet it terrified him too, as Mrs Dimbleby's cloud had done. He touched it gingerly, and a scent came out of it like Easter morning, and he heard the distant music of the spheres. He mustered all his strength, for he was shaking, and picked up the clothes. As he did so his own rags shrivelled away, and he thrust thin naked limbs into the unaccustomed garments. Even as he put them on, however, the mortal cloth thinned, and formed itself into a part of him. He stood up, thin and a little taller than he had been, glowing in the red firelight. Then a dreadful heat shot through him, not like the pleasant external warmth which he had felt from fire or sun, but the consuming heat within, running through all his veins, which humans carry about with them all their lives, burning up their youth into old age within the span of a few short years. A few moments after the heat a weight came upon him which bore him to the ground. It was a weight of care and sorrow, and a doubleness of mind which seemed to be cutting him into two. But this only lasted a moment, for it seemed that something reached down and thrust the weight aside; and his own good deeds, so patiently performed for so many hundred years, reached up towards it, and drew him to his feet. It seemed as if the weight was still there, in the air all around, but it no longer pressed on him, he moved freely within an invisible tower, which moved with him. He ran and danced about the room, blessing it as he went, and his hempen hampen song was taken up and changed by a chorus all about him until it became the air that the spheres sang. Joel and Anne heard a snatch of it, and saw a glowing shape dance past them out of the house. That was the last they saw of Hobberdy Dick so long as they walked this earth, and the cream platter was the last thing that ever he washed; but for all that Widford was a lucky place and well guided in their time, and their children's, and for many a long year after that.